Melani 2

A BBW Love on the Rise

Tyanna

Melani 2: A BBW Love on the Rise
Copyright © 2020 by Tyanna
Published by Tyanna Presents
www.tyannapresents1@gmail.com

Cover designed by Bryant Sparks
BBW Model: Courtney Shaniqua Culpepper
Editor: Crystal Collier

ҁ*Synopsis*ҁ

Melani's life is finally starting to look up on the business aspect, and now that everything is booming, Melani is trying to deal with her inner demons. But the past comes racing back when she discovers the man that ruined her life is extremely close to the love of her life. In just a moment, everything Melani knows changes, and her heart is ripped out of her chest and stomped on. Will she press forward with Javion or will Melani continue to let her past dictate her future?

Between going back and forth with Liv and trying to convince Melani that he's serious about her, Javion feels like he's going crazy. But going crazy for Melani is different and he likes it. Despite knowing the kind of baggage Melani comes with, Javion wants her and will stop at nothing to get her. But soon, a bomb is dropped that causes his whole world to shatter into thousands of pieces. Will he be able to handle the new information, or will he cut off the people he loves the most?

On top of trying to figure out if they're really up for the relationship thing, Erin and Marshon have been swamped with baby mama drama, which only causes Erin to be more cautious, especially with how her other relationships ended.

But this time, it's different, and now having a baby on the way, Erin is more determined than ever to give her baby a two-parent home. Will Marshon and Erin survive this storm? Or is their relationship not strong enough to withstand Hurricane Koree?

Recap where we left off...

Javion

I had been calling my aunt all morning since my uncle had been nonexistent lately, but she wasn't answering, which had me worried. So, we decided to leave earlier. We got on the road after Lani went to visit her mama. Melody wasn't looking good, and she had been in a coma since they'd brought her in. They had asked Lani if she wanted to make any decisions since it was already proven that Melody was brain dead, but Lani decided to come back to the hospital when we returned. Some might think her actions were cold, but I understood why she felt the way she felt, and so did Erin.

"Finally here," Marshon said, pulling up in front of my uncle's crib.

"Man, that seven hours seemed like forever. We haven't drove that far in a minute."

"Yeah, I remember we used to make this trip once a month when they first moved down here," Marshon said, reminiscing.

"That was the good old days before they got grown and started ignoring us," I laughed.

We pulled into the driveway and I took in the maintenance of the crib. It didn't look like the same house I had visited almost a year ago. The grass needed to be cut, and the siding looked like it was coming off. I didn't know what was going on, but I couldn't wait to go inside to see my people.

Once we parked, I told Javion to come in with me. I wanted to go in and make sure they were good with me bringing company in.

"I bet you thinking the same thing I'm thinking," Marshon said.

"Yup. I was thinking that shit as soon as we pulled up. What the fuck is going on over here?" I said.

"Whatever it is, I bet it has something to do with us not hearing from nobody but Auntie."

"I hope he ain't move her down here to start fucking up, Shon. They were doing so fucking good, and money was tight."

Once Shon and I made it up the steps, the front door opened, and an older lady was about to walk out. She was dressed in a scrub uniform, which caused my mind to wander.

"Hello, how can I help you?" she asked with a pleasant voice.

"Hello, ma'am, this is my aunt and uncle's home. I talked to her earlier in the week, letting her know I was coming to visit. Is she here, and who are you?"

"My name is Trish, and I'm your aunt's nurse. She's in the house, lying on the couch. I would put you up to speed with what's going on, but she wanted to tell you herself."

Not liking the sound of that, I gave Nurse Trish a head nod and made my way into the house. Everything was the same from the last time I'd come, but something just didn't seem right. Shon and I walked into the living room and my auntie was sitting on the couch with a scarf on her head. She was half the size she was the last time I saw her. I knew as soon as she saw me, she noticed the concern in my face.

"Hey, my babies. Come on over here and give me a hug." I leaned over, hugged her, and kissed the top of her head. Marshon followed behind me. I then sat on the couch, waiting for her to tell us what was going on.

"Aunt P, where Unc at?" Marshon asked.

"Booby out there chasing that demon. I told him y'all were coming to town, so I'm sure he'll be checking in soon. Where's these young ladies at that y'all been telling me about?"

"They in the car, waiting on us to tell them to come in, but first, I wanna talk to you and find out what's going on, auntie. Talk to us, are you good?"

I saw the sadness in her face, and I knew she was about to break my heart, so I sat there and waited for her to break the news to me.

"When I first moved here, I found out I had stage 2 breast cancer. I beat it, so I didn't feel the need to tell you two about it. I was fine for a good while, then the cancer came back more aggressively. I had both my breasts removed, thinking that was going to help, but it didn't. I recently found out I have stage 3 lung cancer. I'm tired, y'all, and my body is not doing good with the treatments. I was going to call and tell you, but then you told me y'all were coming down, so I figured I would wait till y'all came."

I was so frustrated, I got up and walked out of the house. My heart was hurt, and I didn't even know what to do or say about something like this. My parents had died, and these two were the ones who raised me. Not to mention, she took care of me more than my uncle. He would disappear at times, but Auntie never left me. She always took care of me like I was her own, and to see she was going through this alone because my uncle wanted to be on good bullshit had me pissed.

I was out front, pacing back and forth, not even realizing I was crying until Melani walked up on me. She didn't say anything, she just held her arms open, beckoning me in for a hug. No words were spoken as she held me and rubbed my back while I cried in her arms.

"Come on, man, get ya shit together. We all she has, so we need to be strong for her. Come on and get the girls and let's go in. Let's make this visit one of the best she's had in a long time."

Marshon was right, so I hurried and wiped my face and got my shit together. We went over to the truck and gathered everything we were taking inside. We were going to stay at a hotel, but now I wanted to stay here with her, knowing that she was alone.

"I wanna stay here if it's OK with y'all. They have two guest rooms. I just don't feel right leaving her here alone and she's sick."

"I'm cool with that, bro. How y'all ladies feel about that?" Shon asked.

"I'm cool with that. What about you, Erin?" Melani asked.

"Whatever y'all want. As long as I'm near food, I'll be good," Erin said, causing us all to laugh.

We grabbed everything and made our way into the house. When we entered, I noticed Auntie had taken down all the pictures of her and my Uncle Booby. His ass must have really been fucking up. After we made our way into the house and got settled, Melani and Erin checked the kitchen to see what was there. The housekeeper had just gone shopping, so there was plenty of food. Melani took some chicken out and decided to cook for everybody. While Shon and I got acquainted with Auntie, our girls were in the kitchen, cheffing it up.

"She seems like a nice girl, J. Are you looking to settle down finally?" Auntie asked.

"Yes, ma'am. I believe she's the one. What's really up with Booby? I see you took down all the pictures. Y'all finished?" I asked.

"Baby, me and your uncle been over. When he put his bad habits before me, I was done. I just wished he wouldn't have moved me away from y'all. I missed out on so much, and now my life is limited. I'ma tell you both this, and y'all take it how y'all want. If y'all not serious about them girls, let them go. Don't make them waste their life, thinking this shit is forever and it's temporary," Auntie advised us.

"Aunt P, this is it for me. I've never felt like I wanted to marry nobody until I met her. We have our issues, but I'm not letting up. She is who I want, and she about to have my son," Marshon said, so sure Erin was having a boy.

"Why you keep saying she is having your son?" I chuckled.

"Erin is special, and she was sent to me for a reason."

"Yeah, he in love," Auntie laughed.

We sat, reminiscing and catching up until dinner was finished. Once it was done, I helped my auntie to the dining room since that was where she wanted to sit. She said she was getting tired of sitting in the damn living room in the same spot. She told us she had been sleeping on the couch because she was so uncomfortable in the bed. Hearing all that she'd been going through alone broke me down, but I had to remain strong for her while in her presence.

"This looks really good, baby," my auntie said to Melani.

"Thank you! I hope you all enjoy it," Melani cooed.

Lani had cooked smothered chicken, fried cabbage, white rice, and garlic mashed potatoes. This girl could cook her ass off, and that was another thing I loved about her.

"So, Melani, tell me about this new job venture you have going on. I've heard bits and pieces," my aunt suggested, putting a fork of food in her mouth.

"Well, I just started a business as a stylist, then I plan to start modeling one day if things go the way I want. It's really looking up for me, thanks to Javion."

"That's good to hear, baby. Make sure you keep it going and make every move your best move. At any point, if you feel like Javion is holding you back, let his ass go. If it's meant to be, he will be right back."

"Damn, Aunt P, tell her how you really feel," Marshon said with a mouth full of food.

"I'm just keeping it real. I love y'all and I raised y'all to be good men, but sometimes, men get comfortable in what y'all got going on and forget about the woman's feelings. Then you start neglecting her dreams and shit she wanna do. This goes for you, too, Erin. If you ever feel like Mar is wasting your time, baby, run. I'm not saying he is because they both talk so highly of both of you, and I can tell they are in love, but don't ever put love before anything that's important to you. That man may not change for you, so don't put your future plan on hold because of him," my auntie said, kicking some real shit.

I knew what she was getting at. She had given up a lot to help my uncle raise me. He was in the streets, doing him, while she gave up her future to make sure I had a great upbringing. It was like she became an instant housewife because she loved her husband. She gave up everything for a man who still ended up leaving her for what was more important to him: drugs and the street life.

Dinner was great. We talked and enjoyed each other's company while eating a good home-cooked meal. My auntie was even enjoying herself.

"I'm so glad you all are here. This is the most fun I've had in a long time, and we ain't even do shit. Just having y'all here means so much to me. Javion, baby, can you walk me to the bathroom then back to the couch?"

"Sure, then we can watch a movie together."

"I wanna watch a movie, too. Why don't you help me clean the kitchen when you finished with Auntie? Then we can watch the movie together."

"All right, baby. Let me handle this, then I'll be right in to help you."

"I'll help Aunt P, and you go help Lani so that way, it won't take long," Marshon said, pushing me out of the way.

"Well, while y'all all do that, I'ma go sit my pregnant ass in the living room and wait till y'all come," Erin said, heading into the living room.

Melani and I walked into the kitchen, and I looked for the containers to put the food in as she made the dishwater. I stood behind her and watched her for a second before I walked over to the sink behind her. I wrapped my arms around her waist and nuzzled my nose in the crook of her neck. She smelled so damn good, and I couldn't wait to cuddle up under her later tonight.

"How are you feeling?" Melani asked.

"I'm good, baby, just trying to wrap my mind around everything. I'm having a hard time, knowing she was this sick and been in this house all alone for months."

"Well, where is your uncle?" Melani asked.

"I really don't know. My aunt said he started chasing them old demons again, which means he got back in the streets and started using again."

"Wow, you never told me he was using."

"It was never nothing like that. He would use occasionally, mainly if it was a big baller's party or something. They would drink and hit a couple of lines. I know drug use is drug use, but he was functional if that makes sense. If you didn't know him, you wouldn't know unless there was a party going on."

"Oh, I get it now. Well, I'm just glad we're here and able to keep her happy for the little bit of time we are here."

"I'm glad, too, and thanks again for coming with me. I really needed you here with me." The sound of the back door, which was in the kitchen, opened. I knew it was Uncle Booby since he was the only one who had a key to the house.

"Mmm, Porsha, you got it smelling good in here," he yelled as soon as the door opened. When he walked into the kitchen fully, he didn't expect to see me.

"Ain't no Porsha in here, my nigga," I yelled, walking over to him.

"Neph, is that you?" my uncle asked, pulling me in for a hug. Once we separated, I looked him up and down and could tell he had lost plenty of weight. His clothes didn't fit him like they once did. To be honest, he looked like a crack head to me. Those drugs had him gone, which explained why Auntie had been in the house alone.

"Yeah, it's me. Come over here and let me introduce you to my girl," I said, walking back over to Lani.

"Yes, let me get over here and meet my new niece," my uncle beamed.

"Melani, this is my Uncle Booby. Uncle Booby, this is the love of my life, Melani Clark." As soon as Melani turned to face him, she dropped the glass plate she was holding and started to scream.

"Get away from me! Get away from me!" Lani yelled, shaking and screaming.

"Baby, what's wrong? Why are you screaming like that?" I asked in a concerned tone.

"He raped me, Javion. He raped me. That's Larry. That's my mama's boyfriend that raped me."

ςChapter Oneς

Marshon

After I walked Auntie to the bathroom, we made our way back into the living room where Erin was sitting and waiting patiently. I looked over at her and winked, then blew a kiss. Today had been a day for Javion and I; finding out how sick Aunt P was was breaking our hearts. I was so glad Erin and Melani were able to come with us because they really brought out a different side for me and my boy.

"You missed me, beautiful?" I said to Erin while sitting down next to her on the love seat.

"Of course. You know I always miss you when you're gone. How you feeling, Ms. Porsha? Are you good?" Erin asked while smiling.

"Yes, I'm good, baby, just a little tired," Aunt P said right before we heard all this commotion coming from the kitchen. I hurried and jumped up and ran to see what was going on. When I made it into the kitchen, Melani was standing in the corner, yelling hysterically, while Javion was on top of Unc, fucking him up. I ran over to them, trying to break it up, but the way Javion was going in on Unc's ass, I couldn't get him off of him. It was like he had the strength of ten men. Something had my boy going ape shit crazy.

"Come on, J…you gotta chill, bro. Aunt P is right in the living room," I begged. My words fell on deaf ears and Javion continued to throw blow after blow until Aunt P walked in with Erin.

"Javion Banks, stop right now!" Aunt P yelled.

I didn't know what it was about her voice, but he stopped just like she told him to. Javion got up off Unc and then spat on him. I just stood back and stared because I still didn't know what the hell was going on.

"I'm your fucking uncle. I raised you, and this is how you do me. You believe what this fat ass bitch told you," Unc yelled, causing Javion to run back up on his ass, delivering kick after kick to his side. Melani crying and Unc screaming must have been too much for Aunt P. She started crying and grabbing her chest. I finally got Javion away from Unc and out of the kitchen.

"Man, what the fuck is going on?" I asked.

"Melani said he's the one that raped her." Hearing Javion say that caused my blood to boil as well, but truth be told, we had to hear the story. Yeah, we knew Melani was cool people, but we had known Unc all our lives.

"So, you believe her?" I asked.

"Fuck yeah. I watched her plenty of nights, wake up in sweats with tears running down her face. I watched her toss and turn while screaming. Plus, I know Melani wouldn't lie about that."

"I get all of that, bro, but you just met her. Don't you think you should have talked to Unc about it first? Before you just beat the shit out of him like that."

"Listen, bro, I know she is telling the truth and from his response laying on that floor, I know his bitch ass did it. I'm not sorry for beating his ass; the only thing I'm sorry for is Auntie having to see it."

"Marshon…Marshon… come on, Aunt Porsha just passed out," Erin said, running into the living room. Javion and I walked into the kitchen and Aunt P was lying on the floor. Melani was still in the corner, looking like she had just seen a ghost, but Unc was gone.

Javion kneeled next to her to check her pulse. I could tell by the look on his face that the shit wasn't good. I pulled out my phone and called the ambulance. I would have picked her up and put her in the car, but I was scared to move her. Hell, we were all scared as fuck. I hoped to God nothing happened to her. From the way she'd been talking to us, I knew she didn't have much time, but I didn't expect it to go this damn quick. We had just gotten here to spend time with her.

Exactly ten minutes later, we heard the ambulance sirens. I hurried and ran to the door to let them in. Once they were in, I led them to the kitchen, and they started working on Aunt P. They got her hooked up to oxygen, then placed her on the gurney. After we explained her illness to them, we all headed out the door. Javion got in the ambulance with her and I promised him I would be right behind him. I had to make sure Erin and Melani were straight. As soon as the ambulance peeled off, I walked into the house and noticed that Melani had her bags in her hand.

"What's going on, sis?" I asked with concern.

"We gon' go to a hotel for the night, then head back home tomorrow. You go be with Javion and Aunt P. I'll text you as soon as we get settled in the room. We gon' catch an Uber there, then tomorrow, we will figure out how we gon' get back home," Erin said in a sad tone.

I knew she wanted to be here with me at this time of need, but I also knew she needed to be there for her homegirl. I walked close to her and pulled her in for a hug. I swear I loved this girl with all my heart.

"Y'all can take the rental and Javion and I will get another. The minute you check in, you better text me," I demanded, kissing the top of her forehead.

"Of course, you know I'ma text you. Now go ahead and be with your family. Keep me posted on how things are going with Aunt Porsha, and don't stress, baby, God has the last say," Erin said while standing up on her tippy toes to kiss my lips. I didn't say anything, just gave her a head nod and pulled her in for another hug. After helping them load the car up and watching them pull off, I hopped in Aunt P's car with a heavy heart, hoping that she would be fine.

******

Javion and I had been at the hospital for hours. Aunt P was sleeping peacefully, and they had gotten her pressure up to where it was supposed to be. Being as though she had changed Javion to her power of attorney recently, the doctor was able to talk to him about what was going on with Aunt P. Apparently, she'd been refusing her treatments because of the cost and she no longer had insurance. The shit was crazy since we knew they had a lot of money when they first moved here. Javion had a plan to pack Aunt P up and move her back to Jersey with us and get her started on new treatments as soon as we could. Unc wasn't going to like the shit, but he wasn't doing right by her anyway. We also had to find out what the fuck the shit Lani said was all about. Javion was sitting in the chair next to Aunt P's bed, staring out the window. I knew my boy had a lot on his mind, but we were going to get all of this shit straight.

"The girls decided to go stay at a hotel and they gon' head back home tomorrow," I said.

"Did Lani say anything?" Javion asked.

"Nah, man, she still seemed distraught. You just have to give her some time. This is a whole lot for her," I assured Javion.

"Man, it took her so long to open up to me and let me love her. She is never going to fuck with me like that ever again," Javion sighed.

"I know, I understand, but I could tell she loves you. Just give her some time, man. If she takes too long, go get her ass. At this moment, we need to figure out this shit with Auntie. She gon' be here for a couple more days, so in that time, we can make arrangements to move her to Jersey and talk to the doctor about the best doctors in Jersey to handle her care once we get there. After we get all that situated, we can go find Unc and find out what type of shit he been on while he been down here."

"I don't know if I can be around him at this moment. The way he left says a lot, Shon. I can't believe this shit. The man who we looked up to was out here raping little girls."

"I know you wanna kill his ass right now, but we need to get to the bottom of all this shit first, J. We need to let him know what's going down with Aunt P, then you can talk to him about Lani. Then, after we figure it all out, you can beat his ass again, but let's find out what we need to know first."

ςChapter Twoς

Erin

It had been a week since all the shit had gone down with Lani, and my girl was in a fucked-up state. She wasn't talking to nobody or answering any phone calls; I had even shown up at her house a couple of times and her car wasn't there. I didn't know where she had disappeared to, but I was going to find her crazy ass. I understood she was going through something, but she didn't have to shut me out. She knew good and damn well I had her back, no matter what the situation was.

"What you in here doing?" Shon asked, walking into my room.

"Nothing…just sitting here trying to figure out where the hell Melani could be," I sassed.

"I told you to leave her alone. She needs some time to herself, baby. This is a hard pill to swallow," Marshon assured me, but I wasn't trying to hear it. Lani and I went way back, and she knew I had her back, no matter what.

"I know this is hard for her, but I'm her best friend, and I have her no matter what. So, when I see her, we are fighting. She knows damn well not to block me out. And

I'm not fitting to sit here and fuss with you about my friend," I snapped, getting annoyed.

Marshon walked over to me and sat down, not taking his eyes off of me. The way he stared at me did something to me as usual. He had been at my house for a couple of days, and all I'd been doing was snapping on him. Truth be told, I missed my best friend and I felt for her. I just needed to know that wherever she was, she was fine. If something happened to her, I wouldn't be able to deal with it. The feeling of Marshon putting his arm around my waist and pulling me close to him brought me out of my thoughts.

"I'm not gon' argue with you, ma. I'm about to take you upstairs and eat ya pussy. You need to relax and take your mind off of things, and me sucking the soul up out ya will definitely help," Marshon said, kissing the side of my neck, causing me to squirm.

"Boy, you so damn nasty," I giggled, standing up and grabbing his hand to lead the way to the bedroom.

"I'm nasty, but you got ya little freaky ass right up," Marshon chuckled.

Once we made it to the room, Marshon picked me up and threw me on the bed. Once I was lying on my back, he climbed on top of me and started kissing me. First, my forehead, then the tip of my nose, then my lips. Shon was moving so fast, like he couldn't wait to taste my sweet nectar. Before I knew it, he was already nibbling on my love tunnel.

"Damn…Shon, that feels good," I beamed with pleasure as he devoured my sweet spot. Catering to my body like he always did, Shon was determined to get this nut up out of me. Shon started moving his tongue in and out of me as he looked up at me. The look he gave me did something to me, causing me to try to move out of his hold.

"Aht…aht… ma, ain't no running. Let me take care of you," Shon moaned between licks, sucks, and slurps. Shon locked on my clit and sucked it like he was sucking a piece of candy. The way he handled my body, I couldn't hold my nut in any longer. The smile that crept up on his face as I screamed his name, caused my body to eagerly give in. I shook vigorously as my juices ran out of me.

Once Shon was finished, he stared at me, waiting for my body to stop shaking. The minute I was about to pull him in for a kiss, he kissed me first, causing my body to crave him even more. I felt Shon's manhood poking at my entrance, and the way I felt, I couldn't wait until he entered me.

He continued to kiss and bite my neck hungrily as he entered me nice and slow. He stroked me nice and slow, and all I could think about was how delicate he was with my body. How he knew every inch of me inside and outside. Shon knew exactly how to take my body to different heights. Shit, he knew of spots I never knew I had. Shon didn't do much talking while he gave me every inch. He showed his emotions in every stroke, kiss, and touch.

"You ready to cum for me yet, beautiful?" Shon asked in a husky tone, moving in and out of me in a fast motion. The way he moved, I knew he was just about to reach his peak. I put my arms around his neck tighter and pulled him close to me, so I could whisper in his ear.

"Slow down, baby…I don't want this to end," I cooed, basking in the feeling of ecstasy.

"All right, baby, I got you," Shon said, slowing down for me. We continued to slow stroke each other nice and slow until both of our bodies started to shake.

After our sexcapade, my pregnant ass was good and tired. I didn't even wanna get up to go shower. I guess Shon saw how tired I was, so he got up and made his way into the bathroom. When he came back, he had a soapy rag. Marshon wiped me off, then kissed my forehead, followed by my lips. I smiled at him then rolled over to take a nap.

******

The loud sound of someone knocking on my front door woke me from my deep slumber. I looked to my right and

Shon was knocked out, sleeping. I hurried and jumped up, grabbed my robe off the door, and put it on. When I got to the top of my step, it was like the person got louder. When I finally got to the front door, I opened it and Melani's old boss Cliff was standing on my porch. I didn't know what his ass was doing here, or how he even knew where the fuck I lived. Melani had put me up on game about his sorry ass, and I wanted nothing more than to curse his ugly ass out.

"First of all, what the fuck are you doing here? Secondly, how the hell do you even know where I live?" I snapped.

"I'm sorry, I don't mean to bother you, but I'm looking for Melani. Have you seen her?"

"You're definitely bothering me, and I asked you two questions. Before you ask me anything, you need to answer me."

"I remembered where you lived because one day, I had to pick her up from here when her car wouldn't start," he explained. "I'm sorry for knocking the way I did, but I didn't think anyone was here. Plus, I need to see Melani. I have something important to tell her. "

"Oh, so you out here remembering addresses and shit, but you don't remember you have a kid until she grown.

I'm not buying your little sob story. Melani can believe that shit if she wants to, but not me. I don't believe a fucking word you said to her. Now, I don't know where Lani is and I'll be sure to let her know her deadbeat came by. And if you come here again, knocking on my door like you ain't got no damn sense, I'ma knock you in ya bald ass head," I said bluntly, slamming the door in his face. The minute the door shut, Cliff had the nerve to knock on my door again. I was about to open the door, but Marshon stopped me.

"Take ya mean ass upstairs and let me handle this." I didn't say a word, just sucked my teeth and did as he said. I was still tired, so I climbed right back in the bed and waited for him to come back. While I laid there, I realized that I hadn't found out what Cliff wanted. My evil ass cursed his ass clean out and that was it. I didn't think I could ever like that man because of how he had done my BFF. I was sitting here, cursing myself out about my anger issues. Cliff must have something serious to tell Lani for him to come all the way over to my house.

"What's wrong with your face?" Marshon asked, sitting on the bed.

"I should have found out what he wanted before I jumped bad."

"That's why I sent you up here. I stood at the top of the steps and heard everything ya mean ass said to that man. He came here to tell her that her mama died. Even though that news might not mean shit to her, she still needs to know. Do you have a clue where she could be?" Shon asked.

"Nope, baby…I have no clue. Melani has never went anywhere without letting me know first."

"Well, think of something she wouldn't stop doing, maybe you can catch her somewhere."

I thought long and hard about what Marshon said, then it clicked. Lani was doing so good with the therapist, she wouldn't miss her session for anything in the world. If anything, she may have been going to the therapist a little more this week because of what was just revealed.

"You know what, tomorrow, she has an early morning therapy session, and I'll meet her right in the parking lot."

"There you go, baby! Now, come on and let's go back to sleep," Marshon said, climbing back in the bed. Since I'd been pregnant, all his ass wanted to do was sleep.

ʒ*Chapter Three*ʒ

Javion

Two fucking weeks and I still hadn't heard shit from Melani, and it was starting to affect everything. I couldn't even think straight because baby girl was on my mind heavy. Thank God for Marshon because he got everything set up for Auntie, so she could get started on her treatments. I had put her up in a two-bedroom apartment since she didn't want to live in a big house. I then made sure she had around-the-clock nurses. A knock on my office door brought me out of my thoughts. I yelled for them to come in and Liv walked in. I hoped to God she wasn't on any bullshit because I was not in the mood for it today.

"Well, hello stranger! How are you?" Liv asked, sitting in the chair in front of my desk.

"Nothing but life is going on with me. What brings you over here?"

"I was wondering if you needed any work done around here. I really miss us working together. I know when we crossed them lines, we messed up. I wanna prove to you that I'm on a more serious note this time. Strictly business;

that's it, that's all. I even came to the table with a few events. They requested you and I let them know that I knew you personally. So, what do you say?"

I was kind of skeptical about working with her again, but with everything I had going on right now, I could definitely use someone who knew the business, someone who knew how I liked things run. Of course, I would have to get Marshon to still be involved when I needed him to be. He hated Liv, so I would have to do some heavy convincing.

"Can you let me think about it and I'll get back to you tomorrow?"

"Sure, and for the record, Javion, whatever it is that's bothering you, don't let it interfere with your business. There's money to be made," Liv said, getting up and making her way out of the office.

After she left out my office, I sat back at my desk and scrolled through my phone. Looking through my text messages, I had been texting Lani back to back and she hadn't responded to me yet. I slammed my phone on the desk and rubbed my hands over my head. Just when I was getting her to open up to me, this shit happened. I had a feeling this was it for me and her. Melani would never wanna deal with me again.

"What you got going on in here? I saw Ugly Face leave here," Marshon said with a raised eyebrow. I looked at him and shook my head. This dude always had a name for Liv. I knew he was thinking some bullshit, but I was strictly on some work shit. I loved Lani too much to go back down that road again.

"It's not what you're thinking. I'm not fucking with that girl like that. I'm just thinking about my business. I'm so fucked up in the head about Lani, I can't get shit done. Thank God for you, but I know you got your own shit going on, so putting her back on would really help right now."

"You know how I feel about that, but if it works for you, then that's fine with me. I just don't trust her simple ass. You done played her too many times, but she still willing to work with you. Be careful, bro, because if I see her on good bullshit, I don't have no problem handling her, female or not."

"I'm sure everything is going to be fine. We talked and she assured me that it was going to be strictly work-related. I didn't even tell her yes yet; I told her I had to think about it first. That only meant I needed to talk to you first."

"All right, bro, whatever you wanna do. You know I may not like some of your decisions, but I'ma be there for you no matter what," Marshon said, being truthful. I swear he was way more than my best friend; he was definitely my bro.

We both sat in silence until his phone chimed, letting him know he had a text message. He looked at his phone, then looked up at me with a huge smile on his face.

"Erin found Melani." I didn't even give him time to finish talking before I hopped up from my desk.

"Come on, man, what you still sitting there for? Come on, we have to go get her!" I said, heading towards my office door. Mar jumped up and ran after me.

"No, man…we can't go get her. Erin won't tell me where she is. All she told me is that she is safe. You just need to let her be for a little while, bro. I know you miss her and everything, but this right here is a tough situation for her. Not to mention, her mama died."

"Say what? When did this happen?" I asked in a concerned tone, walking back over to my desk.

"Cliff came by Erin's house the other day, and Erin went to the therapist that Lani goes to and waited outside until she came out. Baby has been staying in a hotel an hour away. She didn't contact anyone because she needs this time to herself. So, Erin told me I can tell you she is fine, but let her be for a little bit. If it's meant to be, y'all will be straight, bro."

"So, you mean to tell me you knew for some time now, but you didn't come tell me shit?" I snapped.

"Man…don't be talking to me like that. I didn't tell you shit because I knew how you would react. Shit, the way you are acting right now, I wish I wouldn't have told ya crazy ass shit. Now, Erin just texted me and told me to tell you." I placed my head in my hands and kept it like that for a minute before I spoke.

"I'm sorry, but this shit is getting to me. I need to find Booby's ass to find out what the fuck happened. I was hoping that her mama would be up, and I would be able to talk to her, but that's not going to happen. I need to get in touch with Unc. When do you think we can head down there?"

"I'ma get in contact with a couple of my peeps down that way to see if they can put ears to the streets to find out his whereabouts. You don't need to go down there just yet; you need to get some parties rolling. Remember we have to pay for Auntie's treatments and her rent, so work can't stop."

"All right, well, after they get back to you, make sure you let me know what's going on. In the meantime, I'm going to call Liv back since she had a couple of parties lined up already."

"What you mean, she came with jobs lined up?"

"She claims a couple of people came at her for work and she recommended me, told them she knew me personally. So, she comes with jobs, too."

"Yeah, that bitch up to something. All right, go ahead and call her raggedy ass back and tell her to hook everything up. I'm gon' keep a close eye on her. I heard she been hanging with DJ Payne's ass, too. You know I never trusted his ass when you had him working for you. Then you fired his ass, so ain't no telling what they got going on."

"Man…cut it out," I chuckled. "Payne ain't got no beef with me." Mar always took shit too far.

"That nigga was jealous of you. I always told you that, but you just wouldn't listen to me. Who knows how much hate he has for you now since you stopped fucking with him. But, I'ma just let it go because you never wanna believe a nigga. Erin and I have a doctor's appointment and I need to go check on the girls. Kira been calling for me, but my ass been back and forth with Erin's ass. I'ma need her to move her little ass down here before my seed is born. All this driving an hour and forty-five minutes away is getting on my nerves." I chuckled at Mar as he complained. I knew he was getting tired of going back and forth, but I knew he would do anything for Erin.

"Nigga, shut up. You know damn well whatever Erin says goes. Now, go ahead and get on your duties. Just hit me up later and let me know how the appointment went and how my nieces are doing."

"All right…I got you," Mar said while standing and dapping me up. Once he left out of the office, I closed the door and sat at my desk. Although I knew Lani was OK, I still wanted to find her. I needed to talk to her, needed to hold her. I knew she was going through so much right now, and all I wanted to do was hold her and let her know that everything was going to be OK.

ϛ*Chapter Four*ϛ

Melani

I had been crying for hours. I missed my BFF, but most importantly, I missed Javion. Finding out that his Uncle Booby was Larry had my mind gone. I just didn't know if we could continue what we had going on, knowing who his uncle was. He had been calling, texting, and leaving voice messages. The last text had me all the way in my feelings.

J Banks: I know all of this is a lot for you and I want you to know that I believe everything you said. I know you need time to yourself, but I want you to know that this doesn't change how I feel about you. I'm sorry to hear about your mama. Lani all I wanna do is be with you right now to hold you and help you through this rough time. I know you may be having mixed feelings about what we have going on, but I don't. I want us to continue doing us when you ready. Don't make me wait too long beautiful. I love you!

Knowing how he felt about me made my heart smile, but I wasn't sure if this was a sign or not. What were the odds of finding out the man that you've grown to love is the nephew of the man that stole your innocence? I just wasn't sure if we could continue to see each other after that. The sound of knocking on my room door brought me out of my thoughts. I got up to open the door, knowing it was nobody but Erin. I knew once she found me, her ass wasn't going to leave me the hell alone.

"It's about time you opened the damn door. I was about to pay the manager to open the door for me. I knew you were in here, crying. Come here, pooh," Erin said, holding her arms out for me as she walked into the room. I ran right into her arms, and we stood in the doorway, holding each other tight. I needed this hug so bad. I had so much shit going through my mind, I didn't know whether I was coming or going.

"Shh…come on in here and let's sit down and talk. Plus, I wanna show you the ultrasound pictures of our little peanut. We are twelve weeks pregnant, which means we are three months. When the doctor told me that shit, I was stunned. I know Mar and I been kicking it for months, but damn, I didn't know I got knocked the fuck up as soon as we started out. I'm glad we're both feeling each other because this shit could have gone all the way left." I wiped my tears and looked up at Erin with a huge smile on my face. I was so happy for her, and I couldn't wait until my god baby was born.

"Twelve weeks, Erin! Oh my God! Soon, we're going to know what my god baby is. I'm so excited for you and Marshon."

"I know, right. At first, I wasn't too sure about being a mama, but after hearing my peanut's heartbeat today, I'm so damn happy, and Marshon and I are doing great. We talked today about me moving down there with him. I told him I was going to think about it, but I think I'm going to go right ahead and do it. That way, he will be closer to work, his kids, mama, and Aunt Porsha." Hearing Javion's aunt's name had me feeling sorry for her.

"How is she doing?" I asked in a concerned tone.

"She's fine. They have her in an apartment with around-the-clock care. She also started her new treatments. They found out that she still has a chance to live with treatments. The only reason she wasn't getting them was because she had no money or insurance. Her husband had smoked up all they damn money." I didn't wanna talk about that man, but I knew sooner or later, I was going to have to.

"I can't believe he's Javion's uncle," I said just above a whisper.

"I know, baby, this shit is crazy. Can I ask you something?" Erin asked. I didn't even say anything, just gave her a head nod, letting her know she could go ahead and ask the question.

"How did you not know he was the uncle? Javion never talked about him?"

"He talked about him, but he never called him by his first name. He would always say Aunt P and Unc or Uncle Booby. And I never got into details about it because I figured we would get to the point where I would meet everyone and know them by their real names."

"Oh, I see. That could have happened to anybody. Now, tell me this. What does the future hold for you and Javion?" I looked at my phone, then looked at her.

"He says he loves me, Erin," I said as the tears fell from my eyes.

"Aww…baby, don't cry. Do you think he's telling you the truth?"

"Yes, I believe him, but how will this work, Erin? This is his family, I can't compete with that. He talks so highly of his aunt. That's all I could think about is ruining their relationship. Not to mention, she's sick. The last thing I wanna do is cause her an early death. She needs him right now."

"Melani, this is a hard situation, and I seriously believe that if it's meant to be, it's going to happen, no matter what. But don't think Javion is going to take no for an answer. I told Shon to tell him that you're fine and this nigga jumped up, ready to come find your ass. Shon told him to give you some time, though. Of course, you know I have to put my opinion in somewhere. Truth be told, if Aunt P didn't know what her husband was up to back then, she can't be mad at you and she damn sure can't be mad at Javion for loving you. The only person she needs to be mad at is her damn nasty ass husband. Javion already showed you that he believed you when he beat that no-good ass nigga up. So, I think you still should see how this relationship goes. You seem so happy with him, pooh."

"I think I love him, too, Erin, but I just don't know if I can do this right now. I don't think I could deal with knowing that Larry is his uncle." I cried hysterically. Crying had become the norm for me for the past couple of weeks, and I didn't know if I was coming or going. I knew one thing; I was so thankful for my therapist because she was definitely keeping me sane.

"All right…all right…hoe, all this crying is for the birds. Call room service and order some food and red wine. I'm staying here with you tonight. We are going to eat, drink wine, and talk. You have to promise me, though, no more damn crying. You are going to get through this with my help," Erin sassed, sliding her UGGs off her feet.

About forty-five minutes later, we were both settled and lying in the king-sized bed, talking, laughing, and enjoying each other's company like always. Until Erin ruined it with her questions.

"I know you don't wanna talk about this, but we need to, Melani. You need to figure out what you're going to do with your mama."

"Erin, I already told you I didn't wanna talk about this. For all I care, you could tell them to put her ass in a box and bury her. As a matter of fact, call my dead beat and tell him to figure out what he wanna do with her because I don't want no parts. Mom or no mom, that lady didn't give a damn about me, so why should I give a damn about her?" I snapped, making my way into the bathroom where I cried some more. I hated my mama, but I felt like Erin was right; I needed to figure out what to do with her.

"I know you're mad about how she did you, but you may need to forgive her in order to go on with life, Melani. Everybody that did you wrong may need to be forgiven in order for you to live happily ever after. I want that for you, bestie. I want your nightmares to stop, I want you to excel in your business, and of course, I want you to enjoy some good dick. I want you to be happy, pooh. So, if you need me to go with you to make all the arrangements, then we can go tomorrow. If you wanna cremate her, that's all up to you. That would probably be the best way since she doesn't have any family," Erin said, pulling me in for a hug, letting me cry on her shoulder.

"OK…we can go tomorrow to handle it. Thanks, BFF, I love you!" I said, kissing Erin on her cheek. I swear I wouldn't know what to do without her in my life. She was my sister/bestie. We forever had each other, no matter what.

ςChapter Fiveς

Liv

I was finally back in the office, working with Javion, and I couldn't have been happier. I noticed that something was going on with him, but I wasn't sure what it was. I would soon find out, though. After setting everything up for the next couple of events, I made my way into Javion's office to see if he was finished with me for the day.

"I know, man, but I'm sick of her not responding to me. I'm missing her like crazy, Shon." I stood outside of the office door, listening to Javion confess his love for another woman. The shit had me pissed. I hurried and got myself together, then tapped on his door.

"Hello, I just wanted to know if you needed me to do anything else for the day?" I asked, entering his office.

"Shon, let me call you back, man," Javion said, giving me a death stare.

"I'm sorry, your door wasn't shut all the way, so I thought it was OK for me to enter."

"You good, Liv. Next time, just wait until I tell you to enter, whether the door is open or not. You can go for the day as long as you handled all you needed to handle. I think

I'm going away after these parties are completed. I may need you to stop by the office periodically to make sure shit is straight in here for me. Clair will be here, but she may need some help. Marshon usually does that, but he won't be able to. Do you think you can do that for me?"

I wanted so badly to be nosey, but I knew this wasn't the time or the place for that. I'd been noticing little shit with Javion and I was sure it all had to do with that fat bitch. I was going to chill, though, and be on my best behavior until I got him back the way I wanted him. I craved his touch every night, but I knew if I fucked this up right away, that would mess up my chances.

"Yes, you know I got you always. Now, let me get out of here. I have a hot date and I need to go home to get myself together," I said just to throw Javion off a little. I had to do my best at showing him that I had moved on and no longer had feelings for him. From this point on, it was strictly business between us.

"All right, well, I'll see you tomorrow, and thanks so much for all your help today," Javion said.

After we said our goodbyes, I made my way out of his office and over to my desk to get my things. My phone vibrated in my pocket, alerting me that I had a phone call. I pulled it out of my pocket and looked at the screen before turning my face up. I was getting so sick of Payne. This nigga would not leave me the fuck alone. I gave him some of this good pussy and now he didn't know how to act. I told him I was working for Javion again. I had to lie and tell him it was a set up so he wouldn't start fussing about me working for J again. I liked Payne, but he turned out to be a jealous ass dude and I couldn't deal with that shit. I tried to stay away, but he had some bomb ass dick that kept a bitch coming back for seconds and thirds.

"What do you want, Payne? I didn't even leave work yet."

"Liv, you think I'm a young boy and you gon' keep playing with my emotions. It's all good when you want the dick and wanna call me, but when I just wanna chill, you wanna give me ya ass to kiss. What, you fucking that nigga again?"

"Look, Payne…don't start ya shit. I told you it wasn't even nothing like that. Javion and I are all about business now. If you want, you can meet me at my house in about fifteen minutes and I'll make it all up to you. I've been so busy and I'm sorry for not reaching out to you."

I knew I was lying, but I didn't give a damn. I needed him to dick me down tonight, then tomorrow, I would decide if I wanted to deal with him or not. Looking at and smelling Javion had me so ready to get some dick today.

"I'm already sitting in front of your crib, just don't keep me waiting long," he said, hanging up the phone. I couldn't believe his stalking ass. I hurried and packed up all my things, then headed out to my car. I looked back at the door and a smile crept up on my face. Knowing that I was here when Javion first opened this little office space and I still worked here with him meant a lot to me.

******

"Mmm, Payne, just like that, baby…just like that," I yelled in ecstasy right before I squirted all over his face. I was tired, but I wasn't done just yet. I couldn't wait to slide down on his big dick and give him the ride of his life. Once I got myself together, I signaled for him to lay flat on the bed, then positioned my body on top of his. When I was on top and ready to go, I covered my lips with his and savored the feeling while I eased down on his erection. I threw my head back, enjoying every minute of him feeling my insides.

"Damn girl!" he groaned, biting down on his bottom lip. I began to move in slow motion up and down as he met me from the bottom, stroke for stroke.

"Mmm-hmm, this shit feels good as hell," I moaned. I couldn't even lie, Payne felt so damn good inside of me, I didn't want this moment to end. I leaned forward and began to kiss him vigorously. I didn't know what the fuck came over me because kissing wasn't my thing at all unless it was Javion Banks.

"Keep going, ma. Keep riding this dick," Payne said in a husky tone, causing me to move faster. I moaned while leaning in to lick his ear. I then began to suck on his bottom lip while I started to ride him in a fast motion. Him moving from the bottom and me moving even faster from the top caused friction on my clit, causing me to climax. The minute my juices started to release; Payne came right behind me. I tried to fall over on the side of the bed, but he held me on top of him in a tight hold.

"Are you good?" I asked.

"Hell yeah! If you keep fucking me like this, I'm gonna have to make you wifey."

"Yeah right, nigga. You know damn well you ain't ready to be tied down to just one woman," I jested.

"I keep telling you, I'm serious, girl. I just don't know why you won't believe a nigga." I believed Payne, I just wasn't interested. I had my mind set on getting Javion back. Payne was not the man for me, but he made the time go by.

"I guess I'm having a hard time believing you because I've been in some fucked-up situations with men. I just like how I've been living with no attachments to anyone. I guess I just haven't met my prince charming to make me believe in love again," I lied.

"Well, from here on out, I'm going to keep trying to show you that I'm serious…and I get what I want, ma, so get prepared," Payne said, kissing the top of my head. My body was extremely tired, and all I wanted to do was sleep. I just laid there on top of him and listened to him talk until I drifted off to sleep.

ᶜChapter Sixᶜ

Marshon

I was now on my way over to my mama's to check on my girls. I hadn't heard shit from Koree in days and it was fine with me, but my mama said I needed to find her and see what was going on with her since Kira kept asking for her. My mama feeling the way she felt had me shocked since I knew she couldn't stand Koree's ass.

"Mama!" I yelled, walking into the house.

"Boy, if you don't stop yelling in my damn house. The girls just fell asleep, and it was hard as hell to get Kira to even lay down. She was experiencing a little pain today, so she's irritable. Did you go see about her mama?"

"No, not yet, mama. I've been at Erin's house; she had to go to the doctor this week."

"I love Erin and everything, and I know you have to check on the baby, but Shon, you have other kids here, baby. You have to try to juggle them, Erin, and your work. I know it's hard, and I try my best to help you no matter what, but Mama got a life, too. I already called Laci and dug in her shit, and she said she'll be by to get Lalani later. I tried calling Koree, but no answer. I called her stepdad and he said he hadn't heard from her. I'm worried, Shon, because she always checks in with him if nobody else."

"All right, mama, I will go check on her after I take a nap. Did you cook anything?" I asked, walking into the kitchen.

Yeah, Koree was on good bullshit. I had already heard that she was messing with some dude. I knew for sure I probably knew him. I hadn't done my research yet, but I was on it real soon.

"I mean it, Shon; you better do what I said," my mama said, following me into the kitchen. I opened the fridge and saw that she had made some spaghetti.

"When did you make this spaghetti, and what's in it?" I asked, curious.

"Ground turkey, mushrooms, chicken sausage, bell peppers, fresh garlic, and onions. I made it just the way you like it, but ya ass wouldn't answer my phone calls last night," my mama sassed. My ass was laid up under Erin and I wasn't answering anybody. Plus, I knew if it was an emergency, she would have called me a million times until I answered her.

"My bad, mama…it seems like ever since Erin been pregnant, I been sleeping like crazy. It's crazy because I wasn't like this when Koree or Laci were pregnant." My mama looked at me and smiled before she spoke.

"That's because you're in love and content. Maybe this one is my grandson," my mama beamed.

"It is, mama, I just know it. Erin was brought to me for a reason. She shows me what it is to be in love and she ready to birth my first-born son." I smiled. My mama sat at the table and watched me while I heated up my food. I then sat at the table and we continued to talk while I ate. My mama knew she could cook her ass off; not to mention, spaghetti tasted so good as leftovers.

****

That leftover spaghetti and that nap was everything. I had got up, showered, and played with my girls for a little bit. The day was damn near over, but I knew I had promised my mama I was going to go check on Koree. I called Koree a couple of times, not wanting to just pop up on her in case she had company, but of course, she still ain't answer.

I parked my car, jumped out, and made my way up to her front door. I knocked several times, but she didn't answer. I pulled the key out that I never used and unlocked the front door. I walked in and turned my nose up instantly when I noticed how filthy her crib was. As I entered, I noticed there was empty liquor bottles and old Chinese and pizza containers. What I saw when I made it to the dining room table had a nigga fucked up. My blood boiled instantly. There was a mirror on the table with coke residue on it from someone snorting a couple of lines.

After looking around the house some more, I made my way up the steps to see if Koree was in her room. When I got to her room, she was sprawled out on the bed, ass naked with her hair all over her head. I walked all the way in the room and over to the bed, then lifted my foot and kicked the mattress hard as shit. Her ass jumped up so fast. When she noticed it was me, she smiled.

"Hey, baby daddy! What you doing here? Erin's black ass finally kicked ya cheating ass out? I knew you were going to ease ya way back home to me sooner or later," Koree cooed, easing her naked body off the bed to stand in front of me.

"Koree…if you don't get ya stinking ass out of my face and hop in the shower. You over here acting a fucking fool, making me have to leave Erin's black ass to come over here and deal with your bullshit. The house all dirty and drugs and alcohol bottles all over the place. What the fuck you got going on over here?" I snapped.

"Mar, don't come in here telling me what to do. I'm grown as fuck, so I do what the fuck I wanna do. My name ain't Erin; you tell that bitch what to do."

I stared at her for a second, giving her the meanest mug ever. Koree was different and I didn't like it at all. I knew it had a lot to do with her mama being gone, but if she wanted to continue to raise my baby, she needed to get her shit together. I yoked her stinking ass up to the point she was off her feet.

"I swear to God on ya mama, Koree, you need to get ya life in order if you wanna keep seeing Kira," I snapped, letting her drop to the floor. "Now get the fuck up and clean yaself up so we can talk. I ain't come over here to listen to you keep throwing my girl's name up every five minutes. I plan on being with her, maybe even marrying her, so you need to deal with it. She ain't never one time disrespected you and she's been nothing but a blessing to Kira in this time of need. Our daughter is still shaken up from getting bit by that fucking dog. She been up late nights and early mornings, crying for ya stupid ass. Need to be thankful for my mama because if it wasn't for her, I wouldn't even be here," I barked.

I knew what I said was a little harsh, but I had said what the fuck I said. It was time I kept it real with Koree's ass.

What I said must have gotten to her since she got up off the floor with tears in her eyes and headed into the bathroom. While she did that, I was going to go downstairs and start picking up the trash and shit she had all over. Thoughts of her mama came to mind. I remembered when she first met me, she hated my guts because I was in the streets. When Koree got pregnant, I promised her I would make sure my daughter was always taken care of and I would never bring any harm her way. So far, I had kept that promise. I swear I would never let Koree do anything to hurt my baby, so she had to change this new person she was becoming.

"You don't have to clean my damn house, Mar. I can do it myself," Koree said, breaking me from my thoughts. She was now dressed down in a t-shirt and some tights with her bushy hair up in a high ponytail.

"You could have fooled me the way this bitch was looking. Now come have a seat with me. Let's talk about what's going on with you."

"I keep telling you nothing is wrong with me, Mar, damn," Koree snapped.

"Koree, you're drinking, snorting coke, and partying like crazy. You haven't even been checking on Kira, ma; something is definitely going on. Now, I ain't gon' sit here and argue with you about it; just know Kira won't be back home until you get right. I heard about you and Joe and that nigga ain't no good, ma. You know I know him, and we go way back. You not gon' listen to me and I know you grown, but I don't want my daughter around him whenever she's in your presence."

"Marshon, I keep telling you I do what the fuck I want, and Kira is not just your child, she is mine, too, so don't think you gon' come in here and tell me what to do with my daughter. If you want her to live with you, take me the fuck to court. Oh, I forgot, a drug dealer not gon' beat me in court. Now, goodbye, Mar. I got shit to do and sitting here listening to you ain't one of them," Koree sassed, thinking she had one up on me.

I chuckled, shaking my head. "Girl, please. I took pictures of everything, including the coke residue on the mirror. You think the law gon' let her stay with her crack head ass mama? Nope. Enjoy your day, Koree, and make sure you call to speak to my daughter," I seethed, heading out the door. I wasn't about to play with Koree's ass, and I definitely needed to meet up with Joe to see what his intentions were. I knew that might have seemed like some bitch ass shit, but I needed to make sure this dude wasn't on good bullshit if he was going to be around my daughter.

I knew Koree wasn't going to listen to me and leave his ass alone, so I might as well find out what his intentions were.

ς*Chapter Seven*ς

Larry (Booby)

Javion and Marshon thought they were just going to come into town and take my wife but they had another thing coming. I was going back to Jersey this week and bringing Porsha's ass right back home. I knew shit had been fucked up between us for a while now. Over the months, shit had gotten really bad with me. The drugs, robbing and raping had been at an all-time high.

I was having a hard time watching my wife slither away due to cancer. That shit had me fucked up, which changed my every now and then habit to an everyday habit. Once I started with the drugs heavy, other shit started, then we started losing money, which prevented her from getting treatments. Now knowing that she wasn't going to be around much longer had a nigga all the way fucked up.

I knew shit wasn't all good, but they had no right coming in here, taking my wife. What went down between me and that fat bitch years ago was none of their concern. I didn't raise them to turn on they people, and she ain't family, so there was no way in hell he should have took her word.

"So, you gon' tell me what happened to your face or not? I need to know if ya ass got me into some more shit," my boy Dre asked.

"Man, I told you me and JB got into it."

"I know what you told me, but it had to be a reason Neph did this to you. I know he not even like that. Now if you would have said Mar, I would have been like OK, y'all had a little argument. But for J to react like this, you must have did some bullshit. You been doing a lot of bullshit lately, bro, I ain't even going to lie."

"Well, this right here has nothing to do with you, and you don't have to worry about anyone coming after you. This was strictly family shit. Now, is you gon' spot me that cash? I need to get to Jersey to check on my wife," I asked.

"You know I'ma spot you the money, but you think it's a good idea for you to head down there? J already kicked ya ass. P is in a better place; you know them boys gon' make sure she good. You need to stay ya black ass here and try to get ya shit together first 'cause if P get her health in order, I doubt if she even sticks around. You're doing bad, Booby. At first, you had ya shit under control, so I didn't say much. Now you looking like them niggas we used to sell to. This is not you, bro, real talk," Dre said, once again ticking me off.

"Dre, you either giving me the money or not. I didn't ask to hear all this bullshit. Once I get my wife and make it back here, I promise I'ma get myself together," I said.

"The money is where it always is, and if you get into any trouble down there, don't call me because I told ya black ass not to go. Tell P I said what's up and I send my love," Dre said, heading to his bedroom.

Dre and I had been cool since I first moved down here. We had developed a tight relationship and he often kept me in my place and saved my ass so many times. No matter how much I fucked up, he had my back and I always had his. He hated my bad habits, especially since he was always the one to save my ass. No matter how he felt, he still always looked out.

"OK, good looking, bro, and I'll be heading out in the morning," I let Dre know before I laid down on the couch.

******

After driving four and a half hours, I was finally pulling up to a Motel 6 in Brooklawn, New Jersey, which was only eight minutes away from Camden. They were my old stomping grounds. Even though I lived in Atlantic City, I had Camden on lock. I even had an apartment in the hood when I didn't feel like taking that hour and forty-five-minute drive. Once I grabbed my bags, I walked into the hotel and walked up to the receptionist's desk. The familiar face I saw was definitely a blast from the past. I looked at her and smiled, then she did the same.

"Well, hello, Ms. Sherry Right. How are you doing, beautiful?"

"It's been a minute, Larry. I'm good, just taking it one day at a time. How are you?"

"I'm good, just back in town to handle some business. Maybe we can catch up when you got time," I flirted, looking down at her cleavage.

"How many nights are you checking in for, Larry?" Sherry asked, still smiling.

"For two nights for now. If I need to add more, then I will. But you didn't answer me about us catching up." Sherry picked up her phone and looked at the time. I knew once I saw her, she would be willing to chill with me, no matter what, and it had been that way for years.

"My shift is over in an hour. I'll meet you up at your room then. Here are your keys." Sherry and I definitely needed to catch up. I needed to know why she was working in this roach motel with all the money she and Barry once had. Unless they weren't together anymore. Barry and I were rivals. He ran one side of the city and I ran the other. This nigga hated that I had more clout than him, not to mention I could fuck his bitch when I wanted to. That shit didn't make anything between me and him any better.

Once I grabbed my keys and Sherry and I exchanged numbers, I proceeded to my room. I needed a shower and some coke so I could relax. If Sherry was anything like she used to be, then I knew she was going to come up here and fuck my brains out.

An hour later, I was lying on the bed, going through my phone. I had got a call from one of my peoples that always kept their ears to the streets. They told me that Marshon had somebody asking around about me. These little niggas were up to something and I needed to find out what the fuck it was. J and I had already gotten into it over that fat bitch Melani. I needed to find Melody's crack head ass to find out where that big hoe lived so I could give her some more of this dick. She was grown now, so I bet she could do all types of tricks on this dick.

The sound of knocking on the door brought me out of my thoughts. I hopped up right away, knowing it was Sherry. I opened the door and she was standing there with a bottle of Henny and some pre-rolled joints. I smiled at her and moved to the side to let her in. I was dressed in a pair of boxer briefs with no shirt on.

"So, what's been going on, Larry? I haven't seen you in a minute. You are thinning up on me," Sherry said, sliding her shoes off and getting comfortable.

"I've been chilling, Sherry. P got me on this special diet. Since she's been sick, I have to follow the same diet as her. She's been battling cancer for some time now," I said, not telling all of the truth.

"I'm sorry to hear that. This cancer shit is crazy. It took my Barry last year," Sherry said with sad eyes.

"Are you fucking serious? I didn't know that, ma. I'm so sorry for your loss." To hear that she had loss her husband to what me and my wife were battling with was crazy. I felt like my chest was starting to tighten up on me. This was a subject I no longer wanted to talk about, so I walked up on Sherry and pulled her in for a tight hug, then I whispered in her ear, "Let's not talk about that anymore. Let a nigga make you feel good for old time's sake," I beamed. No more words needed to be said; Sherry knew exactly what that meant. She started to unbutton her white work shirt, staring deep into my eyes. I could tell all this talk about cancer had her feeling some type of way. I felt this was something we both needed to feel at the moment.

ʗChapter Eightʗ

Melani

A couple of days ago, I had poured my mama's ashes into the Atlantic Ocean. She had no family but me, so I didn't have a specific place to release her ashes. I knew for sure I didn't want them anywhere near me. For the most part, I had forgiven her, but I didn't want any dealings, so getting rid of her ashes was the best idea yet. I was in Atlantic City, doing another stylist job for Blu. Plus, she had Erin get in touch with me since she hadn't heard from me. At first, I didn't wanna deal with anyone, but doing my job kept a smile on my face.

"So, what you been up to? I've been calling and texting you," Blu said, entering her bedroom.

"I know…I've been going through so much stuff right now, it's crazy. Some days, I'm OK, but others, I feel like I don't wanna be here."

"Oh no, babes, don't talk like that. Whatever it is, let go and give it to God. I remember feeling like that years ago and then I met LaMir. That man changed my life in so many ways." Hearing Blu say that made me wanna open up to her and tell her my problems. We'd become good friends and I didn't see why I couldn't talk to her about this.

"Can I talk to you about something private?" I asked.

"You can talk to me about anything, Lani, and I'll keep it between me and you. Hold on, let me lock the room door so no one will come in." After Blu locked the door, she sat on the couch right next to me. It was crazy how LaMir and her had a whole living area in their bedroom. I sat and fiddled with my hands for a little until I decided to talk. Once again, I had to give thanks to my therapist because, months ago, I wouldn't be able to talk to anyone about this shit.

"When I was thirteen years old, my mama let her boyfriend rape me repeatedly until I found a way out. I hadn't seen her in years until she all of a sudden popped up last month. When she popped up months ago, I learned that my boss at the boutique was my father, and that him and my mama agreed not to ever tell me since he was now clean and had a family of his own. He felt like he wanted to leave the past in the past, which was his past drug life and crack baby, which was me." I managed to get all of that out before the tears finally started to fall.

"Damn, Lani, I'm sorry to hear that, boo."

"Oh…baby, that's not the end," I said with a half-smile on my face.

"I'm so sorry, boo," Blu said with sad eyes.

"So, Javion asked me to go on a trip with him to meet his aunt and uncle who raised him. I was so excited to know that we were getting closer in our relationship and he wanted me to meet his family. See, due to my past, I could never be happy. I hadn't even had sex yet. Every time I got into a relationship and it was time for that phase, I end it, but with Javion, it's different. I finally told him about my past and he vowed to wait until I was ready since that was how much he loved me. So, getting prepared for the trip, my deadbeat comes to my house and tells me my mama OD'ed and was in a coma. Not only did he come to deliver that news, that was the day I found out he was my daddy. Apparently, Melody had his number in her phone and the hospital contacted him. I had so much anger in me, I put his ass out and called Javion to let him know I was on my way. Once I got over there, he took my mind off of everything like always. He held me in his arms all night and I felt so comfortable with him. We woke up the next day and went ahead on our road trip. He tried to talk me into going to see about my mama, but I didn't want anything to ruin the trip. I didn't wanna revisit the whole situation, but we get to

Virginia and I find out that his Uncle Booby was Larry, my mama's ex that raped me," I managed to get out, crying hysterically.

"Oh, my goodness, Lani," Blu said, pulling me in for a hug.

"How could we ever be in a relationship? I don't wanna come between him and his family. How could I compete with that?" I cried as Blu continued to hold me.

Blu pulled away from me and looked me in the eyes. "True love always wins, baby. If he loves you the way he says he does, he is not going to let anything ruin what y'all got going on. You've been through so much this past month, and I got you over here working. I feel so bad. You don't have to do this if you don't want to. I'll just figure it out myself," Blu said, wiping the tears from her eyes.

"Blu, that's nonsense… I'm here, so I got you. Plus, it takes my mind off of things. So, you say this is another fundraiser?" I asked, getting back into work mode.

"Yes, but let me say one thing before you get started on that, then I'ma leave the subject alone. If Javion says he loves you and he's still willing to be with you after all of this, let him. A man that can love and cherish a broken woman is a man that is everything and don't you ever forget that. I have a past of my own and LaMir came in and washed that past right away. He came in and vowed to make all my future memories with him be nothing but special moments and he has truly stuck to his words. Love and sex are wonderful, especially with the man that loves you," Blu said, pulling me in for a hug. I knew this was going to be hard, but Blu, Erin, and my therapist had all said similar things and I guess it was about time I took heed. Once Blu and I stopped hugging, I went back to figuring out what she was going to wear for this event.

******

When I was finished with Blu, I went back to my hotel room. I was drained from crying, but I couldn't sleep, so I decided to pull up my emails for my business that I had been neglecting since all of this had been going on. "Styles by Lani" was my everything, and it was time I put my all into it. Then I would work on my personal life. Seeing an email from Nubia Lee had me so happy, but I prayed that it wasn't from too long ago.

Hello Melani,

I'm going out of town for a week and I need a stylist to travel with me. I know this is late notice, so I'm willing to pay for your flight and whatever else you need for you to take this trip with me. I'll be leaving for Miami in three days. If you're able to attend, please contact me right away. I'm willing to pay top dollar, too.

Love,

Nubia Lee

Excitement came over me and I was all for it. The crazy part was, I had never flown anywhere before or gone this far without my BFF traveling with me. I needed this trip, and I was damn sure going to take it. This could really help with my business. Not to mention, she was paying for it. I hit reply, telling her I was all for it and to tell me where to meet her in a couple of days. I would contact Erin to let her know I was going out of town for a week. I was so happy about this, I continued to look through my emails and saw I had a couple more jobs to do and they were after the trip, which made me even more excited. They were both women who had saw Blu at the last event I styled her for. With Blu's husband being one of the richest men in Jersey, she attended all types of events. After I finished replying to all of the emails and sending invoices, I laid down with a smile on my face, something that had been hard for me to do lately.

ςChapter Nineς

Erin

Hearing Marshon's front door open brought me from my thoughts. I was in the kitchen, preparing us something to eat. I had called him an hour ago to let him know I had just arrived at his house. He told me he had business to take care of and to make myself at home. I looked in his fridge and he had chicken, so I decided to take it out to cook us something to eat. I wasn't the best cook, but I could fry some chicken. After I took the chicken out of the grease and placed it into the strainer, then turned the stove off, I walked into the living room to greet my man.

"Hello, baby! Are you OK?" I asked. The look on his face told me he wasn't having a good day.

"That damn Koree. I don't know what the fuck I'm going to do with her ass. She is on good bullshit once again. I don't know if I can let Kira move back with her. I just can't risk something happening to my daughter. I wouldn't be able to live with that shit." I knew whatever was going on was doing something to Marshon and I knew his girls were his lifeline and he would kill anyone that stood in the way of their safety.

"Well, baby, calm down and go shower. When you get out, dinner will be ready, and we can talk then," I assured Shon, standing on my tippy toes and kissing his lips. He headed up the steps and I walked back into the kitchen to finish preparing my sides, which was broccoli with cheese sauce and white rice.

Forty-five minutes later, dinner was done, and our plates were fixed. As soon as I was about to call Marshon, he walked into the kitchen. I could tell he still wasn't in the mood, but the last thing I was going to do was let my man go to bed upset.

"Thank you, baby! You didn't have to do all of this. You could have put your feet up and we could have ordered out. I know you be tired, and my baby be having you sick."

"I'm good today, Shon, and I don't mind doing for you sometimes. Where are the girls at? When are you going to start bringing them home with you?"

"When I stop doing business in the streets, which is real soon. I'm actually glad you came down tonight. I wanna talk to you about what I should do with this house. Should I sell it or rent it out?"

"Why would you do that? I thought we were going to be living here?" I asked in a curious tone.

"I wanted to buy something new. I want you to pick out where you wanna live. I also want a bigger space for the kids."

"I don't think we need a new home, but if that's what you wanna do, then let's do it. When could we start looking?"

"How many days you here for?"

"I brought a whole suitcase here; I was coming to let you know I was ready to move down here with you. I was going to work on switching my doctor while I was here. I quit my job and I'ma just finish school, so that I can have my degree by the time the baby comes. If that's fine with you. If not, I'll find a job down here if you need the extra help."

"Ma, chill, you already know my pockets ain't hurting at all. I got you and my kids as long as I got breath in me."

"OK…now, talk to me. What happened with Koree?" I asked.

"I found out that she snorting coke and the nigga she dealing with ain't no good. She's actually been using drugs and alcohol to cope with her mama's death. The shit is interfering with her being a mother to my daughter." I tried not to get in the middle of his shit with his baby mamas, but Koree got the fuck under my skin so damn bad.

"Baby, I think Kira should just live with us. I know motherhood is new to me, but she is safer here with us. I know ya mama would help out because she already does." I could tell by the look in his eyes that he was shocked by my response. Hell, I was shocked myself. I knew we were in this together, and I knew that when I decided to be with him.

"Yo, you definitely surprise me every day. I swear you make me love you more and more. Let's get you moved down here and settled in a new home, then we can call a lawyer and start on the custody thing with Kira. Let me talk to Koree once more and try to talk some sense into her, and if that doesn't work, I'll have my lawyer on standby." Marshon and I ate and talked some more while enjoying each other's company.

When we were finished eating and talking, I was tired, so Marshon did the dishes while I went to shower. Once I was finished, I climbed in the bed and watched TV until he came to join me.

"Are you still up, baby?" Marshon asked, entering the room.

"Yes, just laying here, watching TV. How are you feeling now that we've talked about everything?"

"I'm OK for the most part. I'm just worried that Koree will bring up my past and then we'll both lose Kira to the system and I don't want that. So, I have to figure out how to place all my shit in order before I bring this shit to court."

"Come here," I said in a soft tone.

Marshon climbed into the bed next to me and pulled me close to him. Being in his strong arms always made me feel so damn good. I think I could really get used to this relationship thing.

"What's up? What you tell me to come here for?" Marshon asked, kissing the back of my neck.

"I wanted to let you know that everything is going to work out and I wanted you to hold me like you're doing right now," I cooed.

"Thank you, baby!" Marshon said.

"What are you thanking me for?"

"For making me feel better about the situation."

"No thanks needed. We are in this together, always remember that," I assured Marshon and he pulled me in tighter. He held me and we both drifted off to sleep.

ʕChapter Tenʕ

Javion

My day couldn't have gotten any better. I had just come from seeing Auntie and she was doing better, considering what she'd been through. The doctor said her body wasn't rejecting the treatments, and so far, things looked really good. Then I got a text message from Lani saying she'd meet me at my office today. It took her weeks, but I knew my baby would eventually come around. I still hadn't gotten around to finding Booby's ass, but what I did know was that his ass had found his way back to Jersey, so I made sure Marshon had men around Auntie's apartment. I wanted him to put men around Lani's crib, but hell, these days, I didn't even know where baby girl had been staying.

"Good morning, J. Banks. Your Monster and rolled blunt is already on your desk. Liv said she's running a little late, but she had to stop to close this new event," my receptionist said as soon as I walked in.

"OK, Clair." I had hired her when I got rid of Liv. She thought her job was in jeopardy when I hired Liv back, but I could still use her around. Plus, I never knew when Liv would start her bullshit.

"Do you need anything else?" Clair asked.

"No, not at the moment. I am expecting Melani. I don't know what time she's coming, but when she does, just send her back," I said, heading in the back to my office.

Once I made it to my office, I sat at my desk, opened my Monster, then lit my blunt. I logged into my Mac to see if I had any new emails. After checking my emails, I pulled my phone out to hit Mar up to see if he had heard anything else about Booby. I dialed his number and the phone rang three times before he decided to pick up.

"Yo, bro, what's up?"

"What, you still sleep?"

"Yeah…I was, but I need to be getting up anyway. What's up?"

"Did you hear anything else about Booby's simple ass?"

"Nah…not yet, but I got men looking out for Aunt P. I told you I got everything handled. Booby don't own shit out here no more. If he come around on bullshit, you know I'ma get a phone call. Dre already called me letting me know, that Booby keeps talking about coming down here. He just didn't tell me exactly when."

"You know Dre always tries to keep Booby in the right direction, but he seems to always fail."

"Yeah, he told me he's done with Booby. He said he tried to talk him into leaving Aunt P alone because she was better off without him, but Booby not trying to listen."

"Booby gon' get fucked up, not listening."

"I told you I got this. Now get back to work and I'll holler at you later," Marshon chuckled right before he hung up.

"Good morning, boss man!" Liv said, walking into my office.

"What's up, ma? Clair told me why you were late, so what you got for me?"

"I got us booked for Miami next week."

Hearing her say that caused a huge smile to creep up on my face. I didn't know where she'd been finding all these damn jobs, but shit, I wasn't gon' complain about it, either.

"That's what's up, Liv! You been showing out since you been back. I really appreciate you," I said, being honest. Standing up, I walked towards her.

"Now you know I always got you," Liv said, walking closer to me and kissing me. Before I realized what was going on, our tongues were already intertwined. The sound of my desk phone ringing broke our kiss. I ran over to get the phone and noticed it was Clair. I picked the phone up right away.

"Is everything OK, Clair?"

"No, boss. Melani just came running out and she said to tell you to lose her number." I didn't even say shit to Clair, just slammed the phone down on the desk, mad as fuck. I ran out to see if I could catch up to Melani, but she was already gone.

"I'm sorry, boss. I would have stopped her, but you told me to let her come back," Clair said when I walked back in.

"I know, Clair, it's not your fault at all," I said, making my way back into my office.

"Is something wrong, Javion?" Liv asked.

"Hell yeah, you kissed me. You know damn well that shouldn't have happened. Now Lani done seen that shit. Do you know how long I've been trying to get at her? She finally agreed to talk to me today, then this shit happened."

"How are you snapping on me when you kissed me back, Javion? You could have stopped me, but you didn't. You so busy worried about her and you don't even know what you're truly feeling right now," Liv snapped, then stormed out. As soon as Liv left out, I tried calling Lani's phone, but of course, it went straight to voicemail. I tried again and the same thing happened. I slammed my phoned down on the desk, then leaned my head back on the chair. I was so fucking pissed. I couldn't believe I had let this shit happen. I just got her to fucking talk to me and I had fucked up. Not wanting to be in the office for the rest of the day, I gave Clair instructions and packed my shit to head out. I figured it was a nice afternoon to go visit my auntie.

*****

"That was good, baby. I'm glad I was able to hold it down," Auntie P said with a smile on her face.

"I'm glad you were, too. The doctor tells me how good you're doing."

"Yes, thanks to you, and Marshon. You boys have always been good to me and I will forever love the both of you."

"You know we got you always, Auntie, no matter what. So, how you like your new place?"

"I love it. Sometimes I miss your uncle, but we could never be again. He has caused so much harm to people and I could never forgive him for that."

"You believe what Melani said?" I asked, curious.

"Yes, I do. That's not the first time a young girl has accused Booby of touching her. I just didn't know it was something he had been doing over the years. I thought it was something he got into when he started getting heavy into drug use. But when I saw that baby shaking in the corner like she had just saw a ghost, I knew she was telling the truth. How is she doing? Have you talked to her since that day?"

I thought about what happened earlier between Liv and I. Knowing that Melani had seen us kiss had me in my feelings. I was so close to talking to her and I fucked it all up.

"I had a chance to talk to her today and I messed it all up, Auntie."

Auntie P looked at me and started to shake her head before she spoke.

"What you done did, boy?"

"I had been trying to talk to her ever since this all went down, but she wouldn't. So, I finally got her to agree to meet up with me, but I fucked up bad, Auntie."

"Boy…if you don't watch ya damn mouth. Now tell me what you done did."

"I'm sorry, Aunt P, it slipped."

"Well, don't let it slip again if you don't want me to pop you upside ya head."

I chuckled, shaking my head. "Auntie, I said my fault. Melani came by the office to meet with me today and she caught me kissing my assistant, Liv."

"So, what's going on between you and the assistant? Do you think it's a good idea for you to still be dealing with her when you're trying to pursue something with Melani?"

"It's not even like that, Auntie," I tried to explain.

"Javion, if you and your assistant was lip-locking, that means you had something going on in the past or you still have something going on. Now, if you want Melani, ya ass needs to fix this. Why you out here mixing business with pleasure anyway? You know better than that," Aunt P scolded.

"Liv and I go way back, and that kiss wasn't supposed to happen today, and I regret it. Now I know for sure Melani isn't messing with me."

"All I'ma say is this; if it's meant to be, then it will happen. But you need to get rid of that girl Liv. You can't be trying to make something work when you still dealing with someone from your past. I'm not trying to hear y'all don't have anything going on. She shouldn't even be working for you, Javion."

My aunt was absolutely right. I was going to do these last couple of parties with Liv, then I was going to let her go about her business. While in the process of doing that, I was going to work on getting Melani to talk to me.

Ϛ*Chapter Eleven*Ϛ

Liv

It had been exactly twenty-four hours since Javion and I kissed. I was growing tired of tiptoeing around this damn office because he had fucked up. I was also pissed off about how he felt about Melani's fat ass. I couldn't believe his ass was all up on her like that.

"Did you get the papers from out the copy machine?" I asked Clair.

"No, Javion came out and grabbed them… Can I ask you something?" Clair asked.

"What?" I snapped.

"Why do you always come in here with an attitude? I never did anything to you but be nice. I don't have to take ya bullshit. I don't work for you, I work for Mr. Banks."

"Listen here, chick, I have not said or did anything to you. This is the way I talk, and if you don't like it, too bad," I sassed, walking away. I didn't even know why Javion had hired her young ass anyway. He was probably fucking her.

"Well, if that's the way you talk, it's very unprofessional. If that's how you're trying to get Mr.

Banks, that won't ever happen," Clair sassed. Before I had a chance to say something, the front door opened and a tall, fine-ass dark-skinned brother walked in.

"Hey, baby, you ready to go to lunch?" dude asked Clair. "And hello, my name is Javelle. I'm Clair's husband," he said, holding his hand out. Clair grabbed his hand and pulled him in her direction.

"Of course, I'm ready," she interrupted. "She's nobody you need to speak to, babe. Now, come on, I have to stop by the cleaners for Mr. Banks on my way back." I watched Clair and her fine ass husband walk out of the door. I swear bitches always got the good and fine ones, and here I was, couldn't get the one I wanted. I made my way to Javion's office to see if the flights were booked for Miami.

When I walked into his office, he was in his chair with his head leaned back like he was in deep thought. This had been the norm for him lately, and I was sick and tired of seeing him in his feelings over Melani.

"Hey, wanted to know if you booked the flights and hotel for Miami?"

"Yes, Clair handled everything, and she booked your hotel room as well."

"We doing a suite together like we usually do?" I asked, trying my luck.

"No, Liv. I keep telling you it's strictly business now. Nothing more, nothing less. That kiss the other day meant nothing and it was something that shouldn't have happened. Melani is who I'm checking for, and as soon as she's not mad at me anymore, I plan to fix this shit. Now, I'm willing to continue to work these next couple of parties with you that you booked recently, but after that, I think we should go our separate ways."

"Javion, I've already told you that I'm OK with this just being work and only work. You act like this is just my fault. Shit, you kissed me the fuck back. Maybe you should check yourself to make sure Melani is what you really want. If it's OK with you, I think I need to leave for the day. I'll see you tomorrow to take care of the finishing touches before we head out to Miami in a couple of days." Javion didn't even say anything, he just waved me off. This nigga was really feeling this fat bitch and I was going to find a way to end their shit before it even got started.

*****

Since it was nice out, I decided to head over to Tanger Outlets to get some stuff to take to Miami with me. This was a business trip, but I was also going to have some fun. After I parked, I jumped out and made my way into the first store.

"You really saw him kissing her?" I heard a familiar voice from behind.

"Yes, do you believe that? All he's been messaging me is that he loves me, he wants to make this work, and how sorry he is about the shit with his Uncle Booby, then I see him kiss her ugly ass."

I peeked around my car so Melani and her black ass best friend didn't see me. I was heated and wanted to say something, but I stayed quiet and listened to her and her friend talk while they loaded the car.

"I can't believe this shit. I'm going to have to get Marshon to talk to his sorry ass. He don't need that bitch working for him if they can't keep their hands off each other."

"That's what I'm saying. I'm already having a hard time dealing with the fact that Larry is his fucking uncle. Like, I already have a lot to deal with if I decide to make it official. I think I'm finished with this relationship stuff, Erin."

"Hold on, Lani, don't you think you should hear him out and see what he talking about? Plus, don't you love him?" Erin asked.

"I mean, I love him, Erin, but I'm just so hurt right now. I don't know what to do," Lani said, placing the last bag in the trunk.

I couldn't believe what I was hearing. These two must have really gotten close the little bit of time they were dealing with each other. I had to think, and I needed to do it fast. Hearing about Uncle Booby, I wondered if he was in town. I wanted to know what he had to do with all of this. I hid behind my car door until they got in the car and peeled off. I didn't want them to see me. I had some shit to find out, so I pulled out my phone and put a note in it to call my cousin Rex as soon as I left the outlets. I needed him to find Uncle Booby for me. I wanted to know what the hell he had to do with what was going on with Lani and Javion.

"Why you didn't tell me you were coming shopping?" Payne said, scaring the shit out of me.

"Dammit, you scared the fuck out of me. What, are you following me around, Payne?" I snapped.

"Girl, ain't nobody following you. I came here to grab some things and I saw you across the parking lot. So, I decided to come over and see what you were getting into."

Payne was starting to be a pain in my ass. It was like he was on some stalker shit, just popping up out of nowhere, and the shit was starting to annoy me. I wasn't going to trip, though. Since he was here, I could spend his money instead of my own.

"I was just going in to do a little shopping since I'm going to Miami."

"What the fuck you mean, you going to Miami? I thought we talked about this, Liv," Payne fussed.

"Come on, Payne, don't start that jealous shit. I told you it's nothing but work between Javion and me. I don't know why you just won't believe me," I said, rolling my eyes.

"Man, Liv, I ain't no dummy and I know how you two be. I didn't even want you going back to work for that sucka ass nigga. I keep telling you to stop playing with me, ma. Let some shit pop off between y'all two and I hear about it; I'ma kill both of y'all and I mean that shit," Payne said in a cold tone. I mean, he'd been mad and jealous before, but this right here took the cake. I wasn't scared of Payne's ass; this nigga just didn't know how crazy my ass was. I wanted Javion and that was what I was going to get. If I didn't, I'd make sure his ass ain't happy with puff girl.

"Payne, I already told you it ain't nothing like that, so please don't start. Now, come on, let's go do some shopping and eat some lunch."

"Oh, so now you cool with me being here. Ya little ass think you slick. You ready to go spend my cash, huh?" Payne said with a huge smile on his face.

"Nigga, please, I got my own money," I sassed, shaking my head at him.

"I know you do, but when you with me, you can keep that shit in your pocket. Now, let's go before we get back in ya car and I put something in that smart mouth of yours." I didn't say anything, just made my way into the store with Payne following behind me.

ζChapter Twelveζ

Larry (Booby)

I had finally made it to Egg Harbor to check on some of the youngins that were out there. I had gotten a lot of them started before I moved away. I knew Joe would help me in any way I needed. That little nigga looked up to me heavy.

"Can I help you with something, homie?" I turned around and some young ass nigga was all on my toes.

"For starters, young boy, you can give me ten feet, then we can talk," I snapped. One thing I hated was a nigga acting like he was hard, and he was the weakest link, which was why his ass was outside, being a fucking lookout.

"Don't talk to me like that, old man. You ain't the fuck from around here, so don't come up on the block, acting like you run shit," he snapped.

I pulled my gun out so fast and placed it at the side of his head. "You gon' do me a favor and pull out your phone and call ya boss. I wanna speak to whoever he is. I'm sure he knows me. Tell him Booby out here and needs to rap with him about something." I didn't know who his boss was, but like I said before, I used to run this shit around here, so I knew it was someone I knew. His scared ass did what he was told, then placed his phone back in his pocket. A couple minutes later, Joe and Heavy came out. Just like I knew, two of the young boys I helped groom.

"Well, if it ain't Big Booby," Joe said, holding his hand out to pull me in for a one-arm hug, followed by Heavy doing the same. I placed my gun back in the small of my back and hugged them both. The scared ass young boy just stood there, looking dumb as hell. They had his ass trained good, though; he didn't move a bit, just stood there.

"What up, old man? Haven't seen you around these parts in years. I thought you were doing big things in VA," Heavy said.

"I'm doing good, fellas. I'm in town for a little bit and I'ma need y'all help. Who running things out here?" I asked.

"Well, you know we got this part on lock, but of course, Marshon ugly ass got everything else on lock. I'll be glad when I get his bitch ass out of here," Joe said.

"Well, word on the streets is, he about to turn legit, so Joe and I about to put the moves on shit. You want in, big homie?" Heavy asked.

"Nah, I'm good, youngin. I'm taking my ass back to VA in a little bit. Can we go talk somewhere? I need some privacy," I asked, not wanting to stand outside and talk.

"Come on, follow us in the crib. And Donte', why the fuck you standing there looking stupid? Go do something with yaself," Joe snapped and I laughed.

"He's a little weak-ass nigga. I hope y'all not trusting him with ya lives," I chuckled.

"Man, chill out, that's my little brother," Joe said, shaking his head.

We walked into the house and there were a couple more dudes inside. We walked right past them and headed into a room in the back of the house. On our way, we walked past a room where all the bitches were naked inside, handling the drugs. My eyes lit the fuck up. Naked chicks and a table full of coke had me ready to go in, but I knew this wasn't the time or place. I needed to see if these niggas knew anything about what Marshon had going on. I knew if they knew where he lived, there was a chance that was where my wife was.

"So, what's going on, old man? You good? You look a little thin, my man," Heavy said.

"I'm good. P and I changed our eating habits since she has cancer. That's why I'm here; I need to know where she at. J. Banks and Shon came to VA on some bullshit, and when they came back, they brought my wife. I want her back home with me, so that's why I'm here. Do y'all know where that nigga lay his head?"

"I'm not sure about that. I be fucking his baby mama on the regular, so I could find out all you need to know, but I don't want no drama coming back to me, Booby. We never really cared for each other, but we never kept any beef. We all just out here trying to make a living. That's it, that's all."

"It won't be no beef, youngin. I just wanna see what's mine and that's my wife. After I get all I need from you, I'll be on my way. Shon won't know it came from you, trust me. It's plenty niggas out here I know that don't mind talking."

"Well, tell me what's really going on. I can't see ya folks just coming down to VA and regulating shit. I know you, Booby; what the fuck is really going on? Why Ms. P come down here willingly? I know damn well they didn't just grab her up and bring her here without ya consent," Joe asked, being nosey.

"J and I got into it over some bullshit. His new bitch lying, talking about I raped her when she was little. Man, since when I ever had to rape somebody? I was the man and still is the man. I could get any bitch I want. But once she said what she said, me and him got into a fight and they ended up having to take my wife to the hospital."

"Wow, that's deep! So, how you know ya wife didn't up and leave ya ass?" Heavy asked.

These two were getting on my damn nerves with all the fucking questions. Once I had the information I needed, I was going to leave their asses the fuck alone. I had helped these niggas become who they were today and they wanna give me the third degree.

"Come on now with all the questions and shit, youngins. Y'all either gon' help me or not."

"We got you, old head. We just trying to make sure this ain't gon' bring no drama our way. Shit been running smooth for us, and we are enjoying every minute of it. We don't need nothing making our shit hot, and you of all people should know what we are talking about," Joe assured me.

"I get it, I get it. So tell me when I need to come back to get the information."

"Give me ya number and I'll call you when I get the information you need. I'ma have to be very discreet when asking her shit about her baby daddy. I don't want her thinking I'm on some grimy shit."

"All right, cool. I really appreciate you doing this for me. So, how about you let me sample some of that white girl you got up in here," I said, referring to the coke he had being packaged and cut up in the other room.

"For sure. I got some right here in my pocket. I didn't know you still dibbled and dabbled."

"You know me, every now and then, I get my nose dirty. So, tell me, where all the old heads at that used to run with me? I heard Barry passed on. I was with Sherry last night."

"Damn, you still be tapping Sherry, but you trying to take ya wife back home? You's a wild bro," Heavy said while laughing.

"When P married me, she knew it would be till death do us part. No matter what we do out in these streets, she still belongs to me and vice versa," I said before leaning over and snorting up the line Joe laid out for me. I meant what the fuck I said. I was going to find my wife and she was bringing her black ass back home with me. I knew they had probably filled her head up with a bunch of bullshit, but I didn't care. I needed and wanted her back in VA.

ʒ*Chapter Thirteen*ʒ

Marshon

I managed to go to Miami with Javion without a problem since Erin wanted me to keep an eye on him. After she found out that his dumb ass kissed Liv, she wasn't beat and wanted me to keep an eye on him. See, Erin loves Javion with Melani and feels like he's what Lani needs. I was sick of her ass playing matchmaker, but I had to admit, Javion did seem happier with Melani.

"I'm so glad you were able to come with me at the last minute," Javion said, bringing me out of my thoughts.

"You know I'm only here because my girl got me babysitting ya ass. I can't believe you took it there with Liv's ass. You told me this was only business and y'all lip locking and shit. What the fuck were you thinking about?" I snapped. I knew he was tired of hearing me bitch, but I was really disappointed in him right now. He had finally gotten Melani to wanna be in the same room with him and he had fucked up.

"Bro, I don't need you to keep throwing this shit up in my face. I know I fucked up big time. I don't know what the fuck happened. We were hugging, celebrating the gig for Miami, and she kissed me…and my dumb ass kissed her back. I guess not getting affection from a female right now had my head in the clouds. I swear Liv don't mean shit to me and all I need is some time with Lani to convince her," Javion said, covering his face with his hands. I knew he was messed up, but I wasn't sure if Lani was going to wanna listen to his dumb ass. I swear I couldn't stand that damn Liv. There had always been something about her ass.

"I hear you, man, but do you think you're going to be able to get her to hear you out? If the shoe was on the other foot, you would be pissed off and wouldn't wanna deal with her anymore."

"All I need is some time with her alone to talk about all of this. I'm telling you, I can get through to her."

"I don't know, bro. She's in a messed-up headspace already, then that shit happened."

"Fuck!" Javion yelled, banging his hands on the hotel table.

"Nigga, calm ya ass down. Maybe you can meet up with her while we out here."

"What you mean, maybe I can meet up with her?" Javion's eyes lit up, causing me to laugh.

"A little birdie told me she is right out here on South Beach with us. She had to do a styling job for Nubia Lee."

"You're lying. How did this slip past me? I have to find out what hotel she's in. Can you ask Erin for me, bro?" Javion asked with excitement.

"Calm down, bro, and you know damn well Erin not gon' tell us shit. I'm sure we will run into her while we down here. You know Nubia gon' be out this bitch partying. Hell, she might be going to the party we are doing. It's some celebrity chick, right?"

"Yeah, some chick named Cloe' Breeze. She designs dresses or some shit. It's her thirtieth birthday."

"Yup, Nubia is going to that shit, watch what I tell you. So, since the party is tomorrow, what we getting into tonight? I need some drinks and some of this fresh Miami air," I asked.

"We can do whatever you want, bro, but first, we have to go check out the beach where the party is going to be held and make sure Liv got everything set up as far as the tents, lights, and decorations."

"I don't even know why she had to come. You know we had this shit handled. You have the side of the beach blocked off where the party is going to be held, right?"

"Nigga…you weren't even coming at first, remember? And yes, it's blocked off. As a matter of fact, I think the whole beach is blocked off. I had to call Kesha in on this shit, too. Liv wasn't feeling that, but you know Keesh is dope as hell with her decorations and shit," Javion chuckled, shaking his head.

"See, shit like that is why you don't need her. I'm here now, so send her ugly ass back home." I laughed.

"Don't start, bro. We here to work and party a little. Just act like she ain't even here," Javion said.

"Shit, you don't have to tell me that. I act like that every time she's around. Now let's go over the emails and stuff and see what all they had planned out, so when we go to the venue, we will know. A nigga hungry as hell, too, so let's get this done so we can head out."

"All right, let me check on Auntie and you check on ya mama, Erin, and the kids, then we can get straight to work."

After we made sure everyone was straight, I headed to my room to shower. My room was right next to Javion's, so we would be near each other. I didn't know where Liv's shit was, but I knew her ass wasn't far. She always had some shit up her sleeve when it came to Javion. I didn't know why it was so hard for his ass to cut all ties with this dizzy bitch. He gon' keep it up and she gon' fuck everything up between him and Lani.

******

"Yo, this beach is beautiful as fuck at night. Baby girl picked a dope ass place to have a beach party. She also got the right people to hook her shit up. You the truth when it comes to this shit here, bro. I swear you the real MVP."

"Shon, cut that shit out, bro. You know you help me out a lot with the business," Javion said, causing me to smile.

"Nigga, I help, but you be the brains behind all this shit. I say you need to up your description of what you do and start charging more money. You already be doing shit for big people in the business. I don't think it's anything wrong with expanding."

"I think I'ma figure it all out when I get back home. Right now, let's go and get something to eat. Everything seems to be in order and set for tomorrow."

"She must have paid a grip to have them close the beach down for two days."

"Man, she paid a grip for us to do her shit, so I had to make sure she had the best of everything."

"I've been looking all over for you. Why didn't you call me so we could come out here together, Javion?" Liv walked up snapping.

"First of all, don't come over here with all that bird ass shit. He didn't have to call you. You did your job behind the scenes like you're supposed to," I snapped. I swear this girl did something to me every time I saw her ass.

"Chill out, man…I got this. Liv, don't come out here being all ghetto. If I needed you for anything, I would have called you. Everything is set to pop off tomorrow, so that's when you'll be needed. All we came out here for tonight is to make sure the beach was closed and to check out the tents. We didn't need you for that, so you can go ahead and enjoy yourself for the rest of the night."

"You always acting funny when you get around this ignorant ass nigga," Liv sassed and walked off. I just looked at Javion and shook my head. If this bitch didn't have something up her sleeve, why wouldn't she bring one of her homegirls with her? Now she gon' be in Miami, walking around, looking dumb as fuck.

"Why didn't she bring a friend or something with her?"

"She knows Cloe' Breeze; she better go hang out with her and her crew."

"Oh OK. You know what I was thinking. She came down here alone so she can get at you. You know how that girl is about you. You better stop slipping up around her ass before she catches you slipping for real."

"I told you it's not that type of party between Liv and I. Why won't you believe me?"

"Because ya ass slipped up one too many times. Now, come on, let's go get something to eat. Where you wanna go? Let's go to Wet Willies. I want some nachos and one of them slushy drinks."

"I don't care where we go as long as it's food." We headed to Wet Willies, which wasn't the norm for us when we came to places like this. To be honest, I would have been fine with going back to our room to eat. I would have curled up on the bed and called Erin's ass. I chuckled at the thought of how I had changed. I was a man in love and none of these bitches out here mattered to me anymore.

We walked into Wet Willies and grabbed a chair at the bar. There were a couple of chicks sitting down the other end, smiling and shit. I smiled back, then turned towards the bartender to place my order.

"Hey, beautiful. Let me get an order of loaded nachos and whatever your strongest slushy drink is," I said.

"Our strongest drink is called Call a Cab. Are you sure you want that?"

"Yes, I'm sure I want that. What you want, J?" I asked.

"I'll take some mild wings and the same drink."

"OK…cool, it's coming right up," the chick said, smiling in our faces. These days, chicks were really thirsty. They were worse than the niggas.

"What are you doing all in that damn phone?" I asked Javion. I already knew he was probably being a stalker, trying to figure out where Nubia and Lani were.

"Checking out Instagram."

"I knew it, nigga. Ya ass on Nubia's page, trying to see if you can figure out where she at. We not going on no hunt for Lani tonight. We gon' drink and enjoy this food and walk back to our room. Leave them ladies alone. I'm sure you gon' run into Lani tomorrow. What you need to be doing is figuring out what the fuck you gon' say to her to keep her from running off when she sees ya dumb ass," I chuckled.

"Fuck you, man! You not gon' take it easy on me, are you?"

"Nope. I was mad as fuck when Erin told me Lani called her crying. I wanted to come beat the shit out of you and Liv's stupid asses."

"Here goes your drinks, fellas, and the ladies at the end of the bar ordered you both another one." Javion and I looked down and gave them a head nod, letting them know we were thankful.

"Man, if this was last year, ya ass would have both them bitches back at your room. Wouldn't you?"

"You already know I would, but I'm not off that anymore. All I want and need is Erin. I'm done with all that hoe shit."

"I hear that and I'm so happy for you. I want that shit one day, man. I need Lani to talk to me. I know I sound like a little bitch, always talking about her, but I'm seriously fucked up about this. Everything, even the shit with Booby's ass. I swear I wanna kill him for what the fuck he did to her. That shit hurt me bad as fuck when she first opened up to me and told me the story. I instantly wanted to fuck up whoever had hurt her, so to find out that it was Booby fucked me up even more. I still wanna kill that muthafucka. If it wasn't for Auntie loving his bitch ass, he would be dead already, I promise you that."

Hearing Javion talk like that told me everything I needed to know. Lani had this nigga's heart and he was going to do any and everything to get her back. At this point, I felt bad for my man and hoped whatever he did worked to get her back. I knew one thing for certain; he needed to get Liv the fuck away from him because that little bitch was going to always be a problem.

ʕChapter Fourteenʕ

Melani

All I'd been playing back in my head was watching Javion kiss Liv. I had finally gotten up enough nerve to go talk to him and this was what the fuck I found. I was so hurt right now. Erin and Blu never told me the hurt you feel when someone you love hurts you. How the hell do you even go on from here? Is this shit even worth trying to make work? Day after day I found my self lying in bed wrapped up in the covers. With *Changes* by. *H.E.R* playing on repeat, I swear this song spoke volumes on what I was going through.

"Aht...aht... we are not in Miami to mope. You have to get ya shit together," Blu said, walking in the bedroom of our suite. I was so happy she was able to come with me at the last minute since Erin's pregnant butt couldn't come. She handed me a glass of red wine while sitting on the bed.

"Thanks, I sure do need this. I'm sitting here thinking about Javion. My feelings are so hurt. How do I get past this?"

"I mean, I'm not saying what he did was right because it wasn't, but at the same time, if you care for him, you need to hear him out. After you hear him out, I probably wouldn't jump right back into things. I would make his ass work, treat him like y'all just starting out. Make him wine and dine you, take you on dates and shit like that. He has to earn the trust back. Plus, you're still dealing with so much. I wouldn't keep pushing him away, though, if he is who you want to be with. Just explain to him how you want shit to be. If he really loves and wanna be with you, he will be willing to do anything you want him to do. Trust me, when I got with LaMir, he had a cheating ass girlfriend named Tia, and we were always at it. It took her some time to realize that I wasn't about to play with her ass. Liv seems like she is going to be the same way. Even if they weren't a couple, homegirl gone off the dick. So, one thing for certain, you ain't about to give that bitch what she wants. She needs to know Javion is off-limits."

I could always count on Blu and Erin to get me right. Blu was right; I needed to talk to Javion to find out what it was between us. I knew he had my heart; I just needed to work on leaving the past in the past. Even though this love shit was all new to me, I'd never in my life felt this way about a man before. In such little time, Javion had made me feel so good about myself. He had even pushed me to follow my dreams. I knew he had messed up, but he was who I wanted to spend the rest of my life with. I just had to do what Blu said and make his ass work for my trust again.

"I'm definitely going to think about this some more, but I do know in my heart that he's who I wanna be with. It's just going to take me some time to deal with the fact that Larry is his uncle. What pisses me off the most is that we didn't even figure out how to deal with that, and now I have to deal with him kissing that dumb ass hoe."

"I know, suga, and it's all going to work itself out, but right now, we are in Miami. We should not be sitting in this hotel room, lounging around. We should be hitting the strip."

"All right, well, let's get dressed and head out. I could use some drinks," I said, shocking the hell out of myself.

"Oh…so you ready to be a big girl tonight and show out? I'm all for it. I'm out here with no kids or husband. I'm about to have me a good time like my man told me to," Blu giggled.

"So, LaMir don't have a problem with you being out here without him?" I asked curiously.

"Nope. My husband trusts me and vice versa. I know what I got at home, hunny, and I would never mess that up for any of these clowns out here. That's why when you called me, he didn't have a problem with me going with you. If he needs to work, his parents will keep the twins."

"That's good, so how do y'all keep the love going?"

"Girl, that's a story for another day, but just know when I married LaMir, that was who I wanted to spend the rest of my life with. That man is the air I breathe, and that feeling alone keeps the love going."

"I get it, and I love y'all relationship. I hope to one day have that."

"And you will, with Mr. Javion Banks. Watch what I tell you. Now, come on, let's get dressed so we can check the strip out before it gets too late. You know you got work to do tomorrow."

An hour later, Blu and I were walking down South Beach. There were so many people out partying, drinking, and just walking in and out of different establishments. I had never been to Miami, so I was having a great time. Blu and I ate at this Mexican restaurant that had big ass drinks, so we were both feeling nice.

"How you like it out here so far?" Blu asked, bringing me from my thoughts.

"It's definitely the nightlife out here. I'm not a big partier, but I'm having a good time. Have you been here before?" I asked.

"Hell yeah, I've been to Miami a couple of times. One time with Ivory, and then a couple of times with my husband. Chile, messing around with LaMir's ass I done been all around the damn world."

"That's what's up, you just living your best life. A great husband, kids, and your makeup business. Life is definitely doing you right."

"Don't worry, you up next, babes. You about to have everything you deserve. Now, come on, let's go in here," Blu said, pulling me into this place called Clevelanders. It didn't look like a bad crowd; plus the music they were playing was everything. Once we made it in, we made our way over to the bar to have a seat. As soon as we sat down, this Jerome from *Martin* looking ass dude sat right next to us.

"Well, hello, ladies! You not from 'round these parts are y'all?" he asked. I was so busy laughing at that fucking gold tooth in his mouth, I couldn't even answer his corny ass. I swear I was looking around to make sure we weren't being punked. I couldn't believe this dude had come out of the house dressed like this. Blu tapped me on my shoulder, shaking her head.

"No, we're not from around here. What gave you that idea?" Blu asked.

"I don't know, it's just something about the both of you. Two beautiful, cornbread fed ladies. That's right up my alley. Let me get you two something to drink," he beamed, licking his lips.

"Sharmaine, come on over here and get these two ladies whatever they wanna drink. I'm gon' run a tab; everything they're drinking is on me tonight. Y'all need something to eat, too?" he asked.

"Thanks… and your name is?" Blu asked.

"I'm Calvin, beautiful, and your name is?"

"My name is Blu, Calvin. It's nice to meet you."

"And I'ma call you Giggles because you ain't stopped laughing since I sat down here. What's so funny?"

"Nothing, really, you just remind me of Jerome from *Martin*."

"Baby girl, I'm older than Martin, so he stole the idea of Jerome from me."

"So, wait, this is not a costume? This is the way you really dress?" I doubled over in laughter.

"You better stop starting trouble now, Giggles. Go on ahead and order your drink before I change my mind," Calvin said, showing off that gold tooth once again.

"Let us get two Cîroc punches, Mr. Calvin," Blu cooed.

"Sharmaine, you heard the beauty, and keep them coming. And, you know what, I want a Jameson on the rocks, baby girl. So, why you pretty ladies out here without ya men? They crazy. A sugar daddy like me would be glad to scoop ya right up."

"We're here on business. Besides, my husband don't have anything to worry about. I'm going right back home to him in a couple of days. I know what I got at home. I'm not interested in nothing out here," Blu assured Calvin.

"All right now, and ya husband is blessed. I was married for thirty years until my wife lost her battle to cancer. Being married is a beautiful thing. Stay faithful, stay honest, and always communicate. What about you, Giggles?"

"Not married yet, but would like to be one day. I thought I had a relationship, but things are complicated."

"Here goes y'all drinks enjoy." Sharmaine brought us our drinks. Talking about this always put me in a mood, so I took a big gulp of it.

"Slow down, baby girl. That there Cîroc will put you on your ass. Now let me tell you this right quick. If you know your worth, everything else will fall in place. Trust me, if he a good man, then work whatever it is out. Just don't be stupid 'bout it," Calvin said, which made sense.

We continued to drink, listen to music and enjoy Calvin's company. At first, I thought he was going to be a joke, but he turned out to be a nice older man. He ordered us food and kept the drinks coming.

ʕChapter Fifteenʕ

Liv

Javion had pissed me off so fucking bad. I couldn't believe he was acting like this once again, and I swear I hated Marshon. This nigga was always worried about what me and Javion had going on. My phone vibrating in my Birkin Bag brought me out of my thoughts. I pulled it out and saw it was my cousin Nellie who lived exactly fifteen minutes away in downtown Miami. I know what y'all thinking; why didn't I just stay at her house. Nellie had too many damn kids for me. The crazy part was, we were the same fucking age. It was like once she started having kids, she just kept going.

"Hey, bitch, where you at?" she yelled into the phone.

"Standing across the street from Clevelanders."

"OK, cool. Come across the street, I'll meet you at the door," Nellie said right before she hung the phone up.

I hurried and followed the crowd that was crossing the street. I couldn't wait to get in there; I needed a drink. Not only were Javion and Marshon getting under my skin, but Payne had been calling me all fucking day. He was really starting to feel like a damn stalker.

As soon as I made it to the door, I couldn't help but to see Nellie's ass with a pink lace front on. The wig itself was nice, but just not my color. It was long with loose curls and had a part in the middle. Like always, her makeup was loud and colorful. She wore a jean romper with pink strappy sandals and a pink clutch.

"Hey, cuz! What's up?" she yelled all ghetto-like, running up to me. I looked around to see if anyone was staring at us, but they weren't paying us any mind. I pulled her in for a hug, then hurried and pulled back.

"Hey, girl, long time no see."

"Yeah, I know. You be making all that money, I don't know why you don't come down to visit me more," Nellie said, pulling out her ID to enter Clevelanders.

"Girl, I told you I'm busy as hell, always working. That's why I'm down here now, to work. Now, come on, so we can have some drinks."

"I know…come on, let's go find some seats. Hey, Larry, it's just me and my cousin," Nellie said to the bouncer.

"What's good, Nellie? Make sure ya ass be on chill tonight. No fucking fighting," Larry said while shaking his head. I knew Nellie was a live wire, but I didn't know it was that serious. I hope we didn't have any issues tonight.

As soon as we made it in, we found two seats at the bar. The minute we sat down, the barmaid walked over to us.

"Hey, Nellie, what you want, ma? Ya usual?"

"What's up, Sharmaine? Yes, let me get a Henny and cranberry. Make that a double. What are you drinking, cuz?" Nellie asked.

"I guess I'll have a Long Island," I said, a little annoyed. Nellie was always so loud and ghetto, that was the reason I didn't get up with her often.

"All right, I got y'all, give me a second," the barmaid said right before she walked away.

"So, cuz, where that sexy ass Javion at? I saw him in a magazine not too long ago. I didn't know he was doing big things like this."

"Girl, he somewhere on this strip with his stupid ass cousin. I can't stand that nigga, and I hate when he brings him along. Javion and I run this business; he doesn't need to bring his sorry ass."

"Whew, you sound like you super pissed. Ya ass needs a drink…but is the cousin fine, though? If so, I may need parts tonight," Nellie said, sticking her tongue out her mouth.

"What about Darrell's ass?"

"Fuck that nigga. He home with them kids just like he needs to be," Nellie sassed.

I couldn't do shit but laugh. My cousin was something else, and although she got on my damn nerves, I was going to need her company this weekend since Javion was being an asshole.

"Ohhhh…this is my song!" Nellie said in excitement, standing up, starting to twerk.

"Savage" by *Megan Thee Stallion* blared through the club while Nellie twerked and bounced all around the bar stool. I sat, laughed, and watched her while picking up my drink and sipping it. This old dude who was sitting further down from us yelled down to Nellie, "You better get it, baby girl." I looked up and his ass looked just like Jerome from *Martin*. At that point, I'd had enough of Nellie dancing. I grabbed her arm and told her to sit down. I didn't want us attracting weirdos.

"What's wrong with you? I was just starting to get in a groove. Why you stop me?"

"You don't hear that old ass man yelling down here to you? I don't want his ass coming down here," I sassed.

"That ain't nobody but Calvin's old ass. He can come down here if he wants. He spends dough, cuz." I looked at her like she was crazy. I didn't want that damn man coming down here. I looked back down at him to make sure he wasn't still looking and got an instant attitude when I saw Melani sitting down there. What the fuck was this bitch doing in Miami? That explained why Javion was acting a damn fool.

"Fuck," I screamed, flaring my nostrils.

"Damn, cuz, I won't dance no more. You serious as hell about him coming down here."

"I'm not talking about him. I'm talking about the fat bitches that's down there with him. That's the bitch Melani that I told you about. The one that be stalking Javion," I lied.

"Say word… what you wanna do about it? You already know I'm down for whatever," Nellie said, starting to get back up. I pulled her arm and pulled her back down on the barstool.

"Nellie, please just chill. Let's drink and continue to enjoy the music."

"All right, but if you wanna do something, let me know. Sharmaine, I need another double," Nellie said, taking her drink to the head." I turned my glass up and took a big gulp. Usually, I would sip a Long Island, but seeing Melani had me super bothered. I couldn't stand this bitch, and I wanted shit back the way it was before she appeared.

Two hours went by and the club was just about to let out. I was feeling nice and Nellie's ass was drunk as usual. I was just glad this time she wasn't falling all over the place because we had to walk down to our hotel, which was like seven blocks down. After I helped Nellie off the barstool, I grabbed her arm and pulled her closer to me so we could make our exit.

As soon as we made our way to the door, Melani and Blu were standing in front of us. I knew as soon as Nellie's drunk ass saw my face, she would know what was up.

"Nope, cuz, if this bitch annoys you like that, then you need to say something. Let her know Javion is yours and she better tread lightly," Nellie yelled, causing Blu to turn our way. When Blu saw who I was, she tapped Melani on the shoulder. Melani turned my way, then turned her attention back to Blu and started laughing. I didn't know what that bitch thought was funny, but I wasn't feeling it. I pushed past Blu and walked right up to that bitch and pushed her. She stumbled a little, but she didn't lose her footing. She turned around to face me and I wasn't ready for what came next. Melani punched me right in the face. I was so caught off guard, I grabbed my face and doubled over.

"No you didn't, bitch!" I heard Nellie screaming from behind me. I hurried and got myself together and swung back at Melani. She hit me blow after blow until the police pulled us apart. I looked around for Nellie, and one of the bouncers had her and the other had Blu. I didn't know what happened between her and Blu because I was too busy fighting Melani. My face was so sore, I could feel my eye swelling.

"Who started this, young ladies?" the police officer asked.

"This bitch pushed me, and I don't even know why," Melani sassed.

"Is this true, young lady?"

"No, I didn't push her fat ass. I may have bumped into her by accident, but I didn't push her. I wanna press charges, look what she did to my eye."

"Well, Miss, I'll have to take you in. She has visible marks on her, showing that you hit her, and when we walked up, you were all over her. The poor lady didn't have a chance."

"I didn't do shit to her, she provoked me. Maybe I need to press charges on her crazy ass, too," Melani yelled while the police officer took her away.

"Calm down, Lani, you'll be out in no time. I'll be down there as soon as I make a couple of phone calls," Blu said, pulling out her phone and walking the other way. I didn't give a shit about Melani's feelings; I was going to make my story believable for these dumb ass cops. I got placed in one cop car and Melani was placed in another. I didn't know what happened with Nellie, but I was sure she would make it home safely with all the people she knew.

ʒChapter Sixteenʒ

Javion

Today was the day of the party, and I couldn't wait to get shit on and popping. Miami was the place for partying, so I knew this shit was going to be lit. I also knew that the way this party turned out would determine future business. So many people traveled to Miami for the nightlife, so I knew once people saw how this shit turned out on the beach, there would be many more people down to book me. A light tap on my room door brought me out of my thoughts. I opened the door and it was Liv standing there with big-ass shades on her face.

"Good morning, I just wanted to know what you needed me to do this morning."

"Just handle the basics, that's just about it. Then you can relax for the party tonight, especially since you had a long night."

"Yeah, I had a long night in the fucking police station, thanks to your girl," Liv snapped, taking her shades off.

"Man, what the hell are you talking about, Liv?"

"Melani and her little friend jumped me last night. You need to get her the fuck straight. I don't have time to be dealing with no jealous shit," Liv said with her lip curled up.

There was another knock on the door, and I knew it was Shon, so I walked past Liv's ass to open the door.

"Yo, bro, Erin called me a minute ago. How Liv was at the club with some chick with pink hair, starting shit last night and Lani beat her ass," Marshon managed to get out before he walked into the room.

When he walked in and saw Liv standing there, all he could do was shake his head. Liv looked at him with the meanest mug, so I knew they were about to get started.

"First of all, I didn't start shit. That fat bitch jumped all over me. She must have been drunk or something because she saw me and just jumped all over me. Y'all know she mad because she saw us kissing."

"Man…Lani ain't even like that. If she was, you would have been got ya ass kicked. Javion might act dumb about ya ass, but I know you, and you always got some shit brewing."

"I don't know why you don't like me, Marshon, and I really don't give a fuck, but you don't know me, so stop acting like you do. You don't like me, so you always paint this picture about me. If it wasn't for you, Javion and I wouldn't be going through all we go through. All because you got it in your head I'm a bad person, you don't want him dealing with me."

"Liv, go on ahead with that dumb shit you are talking, ma. I know your kind, and I don't want my bro setting himself up for failure with a sack chasing hoe like you. He a good dude, so he needs a good woman that's on the same page as him. Not a bitch that's gon' leave him high and dry if the money ever runs out. Not a bitch that's gon' cheat on him with the next because he makes more money than him. Now, go do some fucking work before I find Lani to black that other eye," Marshon said with so much anger.

"Javion, I'm out, but like I said before, you need to get ya girl in check," Liv said, storming out.

"What did Erin say happened?" I asked as soon as Liv walked out.

"The chick with the pink hair was talking shit about Lani stalking you. Gon' say Lani needs to tread lightly since you're Liv's man or some shit like that. So, Lani looked at Blu and they both burst out laughing and Liv must have felt some type of way and ran up to Lani then pushed her. Once Lani got her footing straight, she hit Liv's ass right in the eye. Then Liv's dumb ass went after her again and Lani fucked her up. When the police broke it up, Liv told them that she wanted to press charges on Lani because she hit her. They had to take Lani in because Liv had visible marks on her."

"Are you fucking serious? Liv's ass is going to mess this shit up for me. Melani is not beat for drama and she told me that shit from the beginning. Man, this shit is crazy," I sighed heavily.

"Man, chill out, everything will work out in your favor… as soon as you fire that damn Liv. It's going to be hard, but nothing worth having comes easy. So, what you gon' do is fight for your girl by any means. Now, let's go get something to eat and chill till tonight. I'm sure you will see Lani at this party tonight," Marshon assured me.

I knew my bro was right, but I was still mad as hell. I couldn't believe Liv had started that bullshit last night. I knew she was lying when she said Melani jumped all over her. Melani wasn't even like that. As soon as I heard Marshon's version of the story, the shit sounded just like Liv. I knew what I had to do, and I was going to fire her ass tonight. I wasn't going to wait till we got back home; this needed to happen today.

*****

The party was in full effect, and the decorations were everything. The lighting around the beach was so pretty. The music was on point and the crowd enjoyed every bit of it. I watched the birthday girl as she smiled and danced all over the beach, and thought, *Job well done.*

"I'm sorry about how I reacted earlier. I know it's not your fault how she reacted," Liv said, bringing me out of my daze.

"Liv, I know Melani is nothing like you portrayed her to be. The shit had ya name written all over it. Me and you can never be, ma. The kiss was a mistake, and I'ma need you to understand that Lani is who I wanna be with, so I'm going to have to let you go. I no longer need your services. I will manage."

"You know what, Javion, fuck you. I'm the one that helped you get this shit started. This party you doing right now, I did this shit, and you just gon' do me like this," Liv yelled, walking up to me, trying to hit me. Security came over and grabbed her up.

"Do you want me to remove her off the premises?"

"Yup, Chuck, get that hoe out of here," Marshon said as he walked up. I didn't say anything, just watched Chuck carry Liv off the beach, yelling, kicking and screaming.

After the incident with Liv, Shon and I mingled around the beach, making sure everything was running smoothly, something we did at every event. We went by the bar, the DJ stand, and the VIP section. Once we made it to the VIP section, I saw Nubia, so I knew Melani wasn't far behind. Marshon was right; he knew Nubia was probably down here for this party. I looked around before we walked away and there Lani was. Our eyes locked, and from the look she gave me, I knew right then and there that she wasn't feeling me at the moment. I gave her a head nod right before I signaled for her to come over to me.

"Are you sure you wanna talk to her here?" Marshon asked, realizing what I was up to.

"I don't care where I talk to her, I just need to get this off my chest," I assured Marshon.

To my surprise, Lani got up and walked over to me. Once she was standing in front of me, I tried to pull her in for a hug, but she wasn't beat. She snatched away from me so fast.

"Javion, this ain't even that, so if you wanna talk, go ahead," Melani snapped, shocking the hell out of me.

"My fault, beautiful. Can we walk over to the left a little bit?" I asked, watching her walk. Melani looked amazing like always. She had on a strapless denim one piece with rips in the legs and red peep-toe shoes. I didn't really care for makeup, but hers was done beautifully.

"Javion, what do you want?" Melani sassed.

"Damn, I really fucked up, huh?" I asked in a sad tone.

"Javion, you know what the fuck you did. Then this bitch came for me last night. I told you from the beginning that I don't do drama. I haven't been in a fight since I was younger. I felt so embarrassed last night, even though I had to defend myself. We still haven't gotten it right since the incident with your uncle."

"I know, Lani, and I swear I'm sorry about all of this. I have no idea why Liv came for you; there is nothing going on between her and I."

"Oh, so you two sucking each other's faces was nothing? You know what, Javion, I have too much going on right now… I think it's best we just let this go," Melani said, attempting to walk away until I grabbed her arm.

"Javion, get the hell off me before I scream," Melani screeched, causing me to lift my hands in the air as if I was surrendering. I had never seen her like this, but I knew she wasn't fucking with me, so I decided to let her go back to her friends. The shit fucked me up, but I knew this was my fault. I also knew this shit wasn't going to be easy, but I was going to try my luck again at another time.

ςChapter Seventeenς

Larry (Booby)

I had been waiting forever for Joe to get back with me. I was so ready to get my wife and leave Jersey, but it seemed like there was always a holdup for the information I needed. All I needed was a damn address, that was all. I was so glad when his ass finally reached out this morning. Now I was parked out in front of his house, ready to go in. I jumped out my car and made my way up his long-ass driveway. The house was a nice single home that sat in the middle of the block. All the rest of the homes were close together like townhouses. So, I guessed Joe or the person who sold him the home must have knocked about three or four of these small ass homes down to build one big single-family home with a big-ass yard and driveway.

Once I made it on the step-in front of the door, I rang the doorbell, waiting for someone to answer. Right when I was about to ring it again, this pretty little light-skinned thang answered. She must have known Joe was expecting me because she called out his name.

"Hello, you can come in, he'll be right with you," her sexy ass said, turning to walk away.

"Come on, old man. Come right this way, and don't be looking at my chick like that. I'll shoot ya ass behind that one," Joe said, closing the front door and locking it.

"My bad, youngin, she's beautiful," I said, not lying.

"I know she is and remember she mine. Now, I got what you need written down on paper. I just ask a couple things. Don't let this get out that you got this from me because I know you going over there on bullshit. You told me the scoop about you and Javion getting into a fight. But, it's always two sides to a story and I only heard yours. I just don't need no beef with them."

"I got you, man. If it works out the way I want it to, I'll get my wife out and in the car with me without them even knowing."

"Oh yeah, one more thing. If you see little girls there, don't go in that day. My girl's daughter could be over there visiting and I don't want no shit going down in front of her," Joe said, sliding the piece of paper across the kitchen table.

"All right, man, I got you. And you said that's Shon's baby mama you are dealing with, right?"

"Yes, that's her. Why do you ask?"

"No reason, young blood. I'ma go on and get out of here. Thanks again, I really appreciate you for doing this for me."

"Yeah, yeah, yeah…get out so I can spend some time with my girl before she heads out," Joe said, standing up to walk me to the door.

I chuckled before I spoke. "I hear you, young blood. A beauty like that, I wouldn't never let her outside."

"Yeah, it's time for ya ass to go since you keep drooling over my girl. I don't wanna have to kick ya old ass in here."

"I ain't trying to mess with ya old lady, youngin. That's y'all young boys' problem. Y'all don't know how to just say thank you when another man is complimenting you on your beautiful lady. They don't always be wanting her, sometimes it's just a compliment."

"Whatever, old head! Go on and get out of here and remember everything I told you."

I walked out of Joe's house and made my way to my car. I looked at the paper that Joe gave to me and a smile crept up on my face. I was going to go check the place out, so I could get my plan in motion. On my way, I couldn't get Joe's girl out of my mind. It had been a minute since I'd seen a chick so beautiful. Man, if I saw her again, I didn't know if I'd be able to control myself. I shook my head right before peeling off.

A half-hour later, I was pulling up in front of the address that Joe gave me. I stayed down the street a little because I saw that he had men standing outside the house, dressed in all black. I sat with my eyes drawn on the house to see if anyone was coming out. I could tell this was Shon's house; he always had expensive taste, unlike Javion. Plus, the armed men dressed in black gave it away, too.

A couple minutes later, Shon's mama, two little girls, and my wife came out. I didn't wanna make a scene, so I just watched them hop in the car that was in the driveway. My wife got in the passenger seat and everyone else got in the back seat. Right then, I knew Shon had made sure they also had a driver. He must have had a feeling I would be coming for my wife. Now, I was going to follow them. I knew Joe said don't bother when there were little girls with them, but I didn't care; I was going to follow them all day as long as my wife was with them.

We pulled up to an apartment building that was about fifteen minutes away from Marshon's crib and I put two and two together. This must be where my wife resided, or should I say, thought she resided. It was going to be hard as fuck to get in here. This kind of place had security at the fucking desk. This was going to be harder than I thought. First, there was the men dressed in black, now it was this. After my wife went inside, the girls and Shon's mama got back in the car, but before they pulled off, I saw another car pulling up. Joe's lady stepped out looking better than earlier with a bag in her hand. She walked over to the car and grabbed one of the little girls out and hugged then kissed her all over her face. Her and Shon's mama had a couple of words, then she placed the little lady back in the car and handed them the bag. After she did that, she hopped in her car. I knew I shouldn't have been doing this, but I couldn't help myself. The minute she pulled off, I did the same and followed her to her destination. I just hoped she wasn't headed back home.

I followed her about twenty minutes away and we pulled into a Target parking lot. Baby girl parked all the way on the far side near a dumpster, which was fine with me; it would make it easy to grab her up.

After being sure she didn't see me, I hurried and parked the car on the other side of the dumpster so she wouldn't see me getting out of the car. I knew women, so I knew it was going to take her a little while to get out of the car. They always had to open the mirror and fix their hair, lip gloss, or whatever it was women did. I parked the car but left it running, then closed the door quietly. I had on a hoodie, so I placed the hood over my head and wrapped a bandana around my face so she wouldn't see me. I made my way to the back of the dumpster and stood to watch her for a minute. Just like I thought, she was occupied. She wasn't fixing her hair or anything, but she was on the phone, which was better for me.

When I noticed she hung up, I looked around to make sure no one was watching us. I still didn't understand why her ass had parked way over here. She hopped out her car but her back was facing me, so I hurried and got behind her and placed my gun at the small of her back while I had my arm wrapped around her neck.

"If you scream or make any type of noise, I'ma shoot you. Then I'ma go get that pretty little girl and have my way with her. All you have to do is follow directions and everything will be all right. Do you understand me?" I said in a husky tone.

"Please don't hurt me! If you want money, I have money. Just take it, but please don't hurt me," she cried out.

"I'm not interested in your money. We gon' get in my car and take a ride. Remember what the fuck I said; if you yell or try any funny shit, I'ma go get your precious baby. I know where you live and where her daddy lives."

I was going to handle my business right here, but I figured why not drive to a park or something. I had more of a chance of getting caught if I did it here. Plus, I would be able to have more fun with her sexy ass. I could tell that me mentioning her daughter was going to get me everything I wanted.

I had just the park in mind. I was going to take her to Lincoln Park. It wasn't too far from here, and last I remembered, it had a gazebo sitting smack dead in the middle of the park. It was getting late in the evening, so I knew the park may have been empty. If not, I would have to take care of this in the car and then dump her in the park. I had the gun pointed to her while I kept my eyes on the road. She wouldn't even look at me; she kept her head facing the floor.

"Whatever you're thinking about doing, I suggest you get that shit out of your head. I'm telling you, beautiful, I'm not the one to play with. I will go get your little girl right after I shoot ya ass for not cooperating."

"My man and my baby daddy will find you," she managed to get out before crying hysterically. I wasn't paying that shit no mind. I was just glad me saying the shit about her little girl was making her listen. She hadn't tried to get away yet, so I knew her little girl meant everything to her."

Fifteen minutes had gone by and we were now pulling up to the park. I parked my car then gave her a little pep talk before I got out.

"Listen, I'm going to get out of this car, and remember, you better do what the fuck I say or lil mama is going to die, and I mean every word I say. I have the address where she be at all the time right here. I did my homework already, so I have a plan in motion if you play with my intelligence." I chuckled, handing her the paper that Joe had given me earlier. The shocked expression on her face told me this was going to be easier than I thought.

After I finished saying everything I needed to say, I hopped out of the car and ran around to the passenger side. I opened the car door and she acted like she didn't wanna get out. I snatched her little ass right out the car while mean muggin' her.

"Didn't I tell you not to play with me?" I asked, gripping a handful of her long, pretty hair and forcing her ear close to my mouth.

"Please…I'm sorry, don't hurt my daughter," she cried. I placed the gun to her back and forced her to walk towards the gazebo.

"I told you if your sexy ass do what I say, you'll be fine and your little princess will stay safe."

"Well, what do you want from me?"

"I want some of that good loving you be giving Joe." I chuckled before pushing her inside the gazebo.

"Noooo! Please don't…somebody help me!" she screamed, pissing me off once more, causing me to backhand her. She lost her footing and fell on the floor of the gazebo, face down.

"I keep telling you to stop playing with me, bitch," I said in a husky tone, kneeling next to her. The way she was lying, face down, ass up, might work better since I'd be able to hold her down with my weight.

"Please, don't do this to me. Don't rape me," she cried.

"All you had to do was listen and I would have been gentle with you. Hell, I might have even fucked you better than your man," I retorted before pulling her skirt up and ripping her thong off. I looked down at all that ass and got excited. I hurried and dropped my pants, then climbed on top of her. The tears that fell down her face kept falling, and her body shook. I spread her legs while she laid on her stomach. Once she felt my fingers go across her clit, she began to squirm to try to get out of my hold. I grabbed a handful of her hair and whispered in her ear.

"Don't fucking move," I barked, and she stop moving. When I placed my dick at her opening, she started to squirm again, pissing me the fuck off, causing me to grip her hair again. This time, I slammed her head against the cement, knocking her out. Since she was no longer moving, I slid inside of her, ripping her walls apart, making myself excited. I knew right then and there this shit was going to end fast. A couple more pumps and I was about to cum. I pulled out and climbed off of her. I then used the bandana I had on my face to shoot my sperm in. I fixed myself and got the hell out of dodge. Now, it was time to work on a plan to get my wife and get the fuck up out of Jersey. I always come back here and seem to get myself in trouble.

ʔChapter Eighteenʔ

Marshon

Today Erin had a doctor's appointment and we were both sitting in the doctor's office. I was getting used to waking up to her every morning and the shit was amazing. I even loved watching her with my kids. She had settled in just fine. She started online classes so she would be comfortable at home while in school. Between her and my mama, they were helping me with the girls while I tried to get all these new ventures in motion. Things were looking up for Javion and I. The only thing that was in the way was him still not being able to talk to Melani. My sis was giving my bro a hard ass time, and I couldn't even be mad at her. Javion had brought this all on himself. I was a firm believer that shit would work out between them, especially with me around, but right now, I was minding my business. Soon, they would meet again.

"Shon, you don't hear the doctor talking to you?" Erin asked, bringing me out of my thoughts.

"My fault, I was thinking about something."

"I was asking what do you want: a girl or a boy?" the doctor asked.

"Oh, I'm sorry, doc. To answer your question, I know it's a boy," I assured her.

"Here he goes with that," Erin giggled.

"So, you sure you are having a boy, huh?" the doc asked.

"Yup, now, when do we find that out?"

"The next appointment, you'll be able to find out the sex. Everything looks great, Mom, and you are measuring the right size. Now, let's listen to this heartbeat."

I smiled while listening to the sound of my baby's strong heartbeat. I was so excited, especially since I really did have a strong feeling this was going to be a boy. I knew if it was a girl, I might be a little sad, but I would still love the baby the same. Plus, Erin and I would just try again.

"Heartbeat is great and pretty strong. Everything is going well, Erin. Are you still experiencing nausea?" the doc asked.

"Not like I was, only when I eat certain things. Before, it used to be everything I ate. Hell, I didn't even have to eat, but I read somewhere that it stops at five months. Is that true?"

"For most mothers, yes, but for others, there's a possibility it will last longer. In your case, since you don't have it as much, I'm sure it will stop."

"OK, cool. Thanks, Doctor James."

"You're welcome, and I will see you and Dad in two weeks."

After the doctor wiped the jelly stuff off Erin's stomach, she left out of the room and I helped Erin up. Right before we were about to walk out of the office, my phone started to ring. I looked to see who it was and saw Joe's name flashing across my screen. It was a shock to me, so I picked up right away.

"What's good, my boy?" I answered.

"Yo, can you meet me at my crib? Koree is missing."

"Man, how you know Koree just didn't up and bounce on you?"

"Man, her car was found in the Target parking lot not too far from you with her phone, purse and everything inside. You know that shit ain't right."

"All right…let me drop my girl off and I'll be right over there. Give me about a half-hour," was all I said before I hung up.

Something wasn't right. Koree would not have left her purse and phone in the car and went somewhere else. I had to find out what the fuck was going on because this shit right here was suspect.

"Baby, is everything OK?" Erin asked.

"No, baby, that was Koree's man. She's missing and the shit not looking good."

"Oh, my goodness. Do you want me to find another ride and you just go?" Erin asked.

This lady never ceased to amaze me. That was why I loved her ass so much. I couldn't wait to spend the rest of my life with her.

"No, baby, I'm gon' drop you off then I'll go. Now, come on, let's head out so I can hurry up." I pulled out my phone and shot Javion a text, letting him know I needed him to take a ride with me, so I was about to come scoop him.

Erin and I hurried out of the doctor's office so I could make this move. Koree and I might get into it a lot, but Kira loved her mama and I hoped to God she was good.

A half-hour later, I was pulling up in front of Javion's office, waiting for him to come out. I was so caught up in my thoughts, I didn't even realize that he had already gotten into the car.

"You good, bro? Where we headed to?" Javion asked as soon as he put his seatbelt on.

"Something is going on with Koree. Joe called me while I was at the doctor with Erin. I don't like the feeling I'm getting, man. I hope she is good," I assured Javion.

"Well, let's go find out what the fuck is going on," Javion demanded. He didn't have to tell me twice; I peeled off with one destination in mind. All kinds of shit was going through my mind. Koree had been in a really dark place and I wasn't feeling it. I figured she needed help after her mama died, but she wasn't trying to hear shit I had to say. Her step-pop came to mind, but I didn't wanna call him until I found out what the fuck was going on.

I pulled up to Joe's house, where him and his boy Heavy were both sitting out on his porch. I parked and jumped out with Javion following me. Once I made it face to face with Joe and Heavy, we all dapped each other up and sat down on the chairs he had on his porch.

"So, what's up, Joe? Talk to me. What's going on?"

"Man, I thought she was on some BS because she was supposed to come back here last night. I was calling her phone nonstop, but she wasn't answering. Then I got a phone call from the police, letting me know if I didn't come get the car from Target's parking lot, it would be towed. It was a good thing my boy Shawn was the cop that showed up to Target when the manager called. I hurried and got there, and at first, I thought she was on good bullshit and had parked her car there until I noticed her doors were unlocked and she had left her purse and phone in the car.

Right then, I knew something was going on. I called you 'cause maybe you know something I don't," Joe said with a raised brow.

"I hadn't talked to her in a couple of days, and then yesterday, she said she was going to bring some stuff over for Kira. After that, we didn't talk to each other."

I sat there with my hand on my chin, trying to figure out what the fuck was going on. I looked at Joe and I wondered if he had anything to do with this.

"You sure you don't have anything to do with her disappearance?" Javion asked, saying what I was thinking.

"Man, come on now with that dumb shit. He doesn't have shit to do with her being missing. If he did, do you think he would have called you? We only called so you can help put some people to the streets," Heavy snapped.

"Nigga, you better tone it down a little. I just asked a fucking question, and I don't give a fuck about who feels some type of way. All I needed was a yes or a no, none of that slick shit," Javion snapped back.

"Come on, y'all, it ain't even that type of party. Joe, when was the last time you spoke to her?" I asked.

I had known Joe and Heavy forever. I didn't really care for either of them, but we all kept the peace in the streets and did our own thing. They ran a small area and I ran the rest. As long as they made their money and didn't get in my way, I was good, and they were good, too. I respected Joe because he never got greedy and tried to take me out so he could snatch up my territory like most of these niggas did around the world. I watched him as he sat with the meanest mug ever on his face. I could tell at this point, he was getting aggravated with all my and Javion's tactics.

"Man, I talked to her yesterday as soon as she got to Target. She called to ask what I wanted for dinner so she could pick it up on the way to my crib. After that, I didn't hear anything else from her. I've been calling and texting her all night. Now can we quit with the third degree and put some niggas to the streets. My girl been missing since yesterday and I don't know about you dudes, but I'm ready to find her," Joe barked.

"I'll arrange some things and you do the same. I'm going to start my own search party and call one of my cop buddies to help with this as well. You do you and we'll keep in touch with each other if we find anything, and please don't tell her step-pop anything. I wanna find her first. He still dealing with the loss of her mother and I don't wanna put that on him," I said and got up to head to my car. Javion got up and did the same. No other words needed to be said. I watched Joe pick up his phone, so I knew he was already up on it.

As soon as I hopped in my car, I pulled my phone out to call my boy, Officer Cole. The minute I was about to dial his number, my phone started to ring. I looked down at the ringing phone only to see Cole was calling me. What a fucking coincidence.

"Shon, I'm here at Lincoln Park. I think we found your baby mama. As a matter of fact, I'm sure it's her. I didn't call anything in just yet. I didn't know how you wanted to handle this. She's still alive, but she needs medical attention."

"Cole, I don't care who you need to contact or what you have to do, get her there. I'll be there!"

"I'll probably get in trouble for this, but I'ma take her myself. I'ma take her to AlantiCare Regional, see you in a little bit."

My heart was beating fast as fuck. I didn't know what shape she was in, but the shit didn't sound good. I shot Joe a text and told him to meet me at AlantiCare Regional, then I peeled off. I felt Javion's eyes on me, so I knew he was going to say something.

"She gon' be good, bro," Javion said, trying to make me feel better, but deep inside, I was scared. I said a lot of shit about Koree, but truth be told, I wouldn't know how to comfort my baby if she didn't make it.

ʒChapter Nineteenʓ

Liv

I had finally gotten my cousin Rex to find Javion's Uncle Booby. I also found out some things about him. This man was a whole pervert and we had learned about many young girls that he had sexually assaulted. I even knew about the most recent one he attacked a couple of nights ago, Marshon's baby mama. So, when I called to meet up with him, I made sure to carry my gun to be on the safe side. I would have brought Payne in with me, but he didn't need to know I was still trying everything in my power to get Javion back.

I made sure to set up a meeting with us in a public place where there was a lot of people. I was now sitting in Kelsey's on Pacific Ave. I loved the food there and the live band; not to mention, Pacific Ave., where it was located, was always busy. I sat and sipped my sweet tea, waiting for his late ass to show up. I made sure to tell him what I was going to have on so he would recognize me.

"Hey, pretty lady! I'm Booby, and you are?" Booby brought me out of my thoughts.

"Hello, I'm Liv, and it's nice to meet you. As I told you on the phone, I think me and you can help each other out."

"OK, little lady, let's discuss business," Booby said, sitting down.

I took in his appearance and he looked like a whole coke head, and I knew he was going to be on good bullshit. I also knew since he had been sweet on Melani since she was younger, I knew her address would be music to his ears. After he showed up and hurt her again, I knew that would seal the deal, being as though she couldn't seem to look past it now.

"So, I hear you've been a busy man all your life. Larry, Booby, Big L that used to run the whole Atlantic County. The same man that loves touching women that don't belong to him. The man that even has a fetish for younger girls as well. I'm not here to judge you at all, but there's one particular girl you had your way with and I want her out of my way. See, I want your nephew Javion, but the fat bitch is in my way. I'll make it worth your while if you repeat what you did to her years ago."

Booby just sat there looking at me like I was crazy for a second before he finally spoke.

"First of all, little lady, what the hell are you talking about?" he asked like what I said wasn't true. I didn't say anything, just pulled out a big yellow folder and slid it across the table. I didn't know how my cousin had found out all he had. I guess he was that good at what he does. I watched him open the folder and look through it. The mean mug that appeared on his face caused me to laugh.

"So, you in or what? You handle this for me, and I'll keep your secret about Marshon's baby mama," I said, taking his breath away. Rex had someone tailing him that day and dude saw everything. Even got a picture of him walking through the park with the gun held to the chick's back.

"Listen here, bitch. I don't know you or how you found out your information, but don't come in here thinking you got one up on me. I did a lot of shit in my life and I'm still breathing, so because you did your homework don't mean shit to me. I just want my wife and to head back to Virginia."

"Do you think your wife is going to wanna go with you after she hears what you did to Koree?" I said, winking at him.

"I hate a backstabbing bitch like you. You's a cold one. You actually want me to rape a chick so you can get her man. I take it this nigga don't want ya dumb ass," he chuckled, pissing me the fuck off.

"Look, you either in or I'll just go to Marshon and the police with my picture of you walking through Lincoln Park with a gun on Koree," I giggled.

"How much money are you talking, and how do I know you not gon' fuck me over?"

"I'll get up a little money for you, not sure how much, though."

"What the fuck you mean, a little money? Bitch, you out ya mind!" Booby snapped.

"Now, now, Booby, that's no way to talk to the one that has your life in her hands right now. Do you know how much jail time you can do if I go to the police?"

"Bitch, most of the shit you got in that folder is old shit."

"March 15th, Alisha Taylor, age seventeen. Shannon Graham, December 24th, age twenty-one. You raped that poor girl the day before Christmas. Let's see, we are in May, so that means these two aren't that old. Hmm…how much time you think you'll get for these two? Not to mention, what they do to rapists in jail."

Booby was now sitting there with his face tore up. I knew I was going to need leverage for his ass, which was why I didn't announce the girls from Virginia until now. I slid a piece of paper across the table with Melani's name and address on it; Booby grabbed it and opened it up.

"Once it's done, you will contact me, and I'll get you your money. After that, we won't have any more contact. I don't know how much longer you plan to stay in Atlantic County, but you have a week to handle this before I turn ya ass in," I assured Booby, getting up to walk away. I knew he would try something, which was why I had Payne waiting outside for me. I shot him a text, letting him know to pull up in front of the door. Of course, I had to tell his nosey ass I had a meeting for a new job offer, so I needed him to stay in the car and wait for me. As soon as I made it out front, Payne was pulling up and Booby was so close to me, I could feel his breath on my neck. I hurried and hopped in the car and closed the door. Then I looked at Booby while he stood there and watched us pull off. Before I even got the seat belt on all the way, Payne started his shit.

"Why was he all up on you like that?" The constant questions were annoying me. It was like I couldn't do shit without his ass investigating.

"Payne, please don't fucking start. I swear you always acting like you my daddy or something. News flash, dude, I don't belong to you. So, it doesn't matter who he was," I sassed. The look on his face showed me that he wasn't pleased with what I said. Before I knew it, Payne had one hand on the steering wheel and the other hand, backhanding the shit out of me. My head hit the passenger side window hard as fuck. I was surprised I didn't break that shit. I also was surprised that he had just hit me like that. I was mad as fuck. As soon as I got myself together, I took my seat belt off, turned towards him and started swinging on him. I didn't give a damn that he was driving. He was not going to hit me like that and I not hit his ass back.

"Bitch ass nigga, don't be putting ya fucking hands on me! "I yelled, still hitting him. The car came to an abrupt stop and Payne grabbed me by my neck and squeezed hard as hell until he got me to calm down.

"You gon' stop disrespecting me, Liv. Either you going to be with me or you're going to die and that's what it's going to be. Now, you gon' calm down or die right in this damn car. It's up to you." When I felt like I couldn't breathe and the tears fell from my eyes, I shook my head yes, so he knew he could stop choking me. Once Payne let me go, he put my seatbelt back on, then kissed my cheek. Then this crazy nigga drove off like the shit he just did was normal. I could see now I was gonna have to kill Payne because I wasn't letting him kill me.

ʗ*Chapter Twenty*ʗ

Melani

I was moping around my place, still pissed off at what happened in Miami. I just couldn't believe I let that bitch bring me out of character. Then the nerve of this nigga, still trying to talk to me about it at the party. That shit pissed me off, too. The party wasn't the time or place for that. The hard knocking at my front door brought me out of my thoughts. I walked over to the door and looked through the peephole before I opened it. When I saw it was my deadbeat, I really didn't feel like opening up the door, but Erin and Blu's voices were in my head, telling me that I had to forgive in order to move on.

"Cliff, what are you doing here?" I asked, taking in his appearance. The clothing he wore was dirty and his eyes were bloodshot red as if he had been crying.

"Lani, can I come in and talk to you, please." I could tell he had a lot on his mind, so I moved to the side and let him in.

"Cliff, what's going on? Why do you look like you lost your best friend?"

"They're gone, Melani," Cliff said right before the tears started to fall from his eyes.

"Who's gone, Cliff? What are you talking about?"

"Evelyn and Elise. They were driving to South Carolina to see Evelyn's mama and got into a car accident. I lost my family, Melani, and you are all I have left. I know we are not on good terms, but I needed someone to talk to. I'm about to lose my damn mind. I've been in the house, running myself crazy. I haven't even been in to open my store. I don't think I can make it without you being by my side. I know I fucked up with you and I'm truly sorry. I know I may seem like an ass for just popping up at a time like this, but I knew if I had called or texted, you would not answer me."

I understood he was going through something since he had loss his family, but the nerve of him to come around now. I was so over people right now, I didn't know what to do.

"Cliff, you're absolutely right. Now you wanna acknowledge me because you loss your other family. That's real fucked up. My friends keep telling me I need to forgive, but how should I feel about you wanting to be my dad now because I'm all you got left. I don't think I feel like discussing this today, so I think you should leave," I demanded.

"I'm going to go ahead and leave, but I'm not going to give up," Cliff said in a sad tone while heading towards the door.

When I opened up the door to let him out, Erin was walking up my front steps. I looked at her and my best friend was glowing with her belly poking out, looking like she was more than almost five months. I knew I was about to hear her big mouth as soon as I closed the door.

"Oh my God, Lani, what happened to Cliff?" Erin asked, not even giving me a chance to close the fucking door.

"Evelyn and Elise died in a car accident and now he wanna be my daddy," I said sarcastically, watching Erin stand there, looking shocked at what I'd said.

"Damn, Lani, you don't have to sound so cold. What did you say to that man? Don't lie to me either, Melani."

"Erin, ain't nobody gotta lie to you. I told him just how I felt. I told him it was fucked up for him to wanna be my daddy now since he loss his family. I feel like it's a smack in my face and I don't think I wanna talk to him about that right now," I sassed.

"Now, why you gotta be like that? It's not like he hasn't been texting you, trying to reach out, Melani. You the one that chooses not to talk to him. I think you're being a little stubborn. Always remember you have to forgive to move on in life. I keep saying the same thing over and over again because I need to start understanding. I want you to live a happy life, pooh. I'm sick of you walking around, sad or mad. I want my best friend happy and smiling."

"Erin, I don't wanna talk about this right now. We can either change the subject or you can leave."

"Girl, I ain't going nowhere; we will revisit this subject at a different time. You already know you don't scare me, BFF, so I don't know why you even tried it. On a better note, we find out what the baby is next week, and I'm going to have you on the phone listening," Erin said, making me smile. Even though I was pissed off, she knew how to brighten my day.

"I can't wait! I'm so ready to start shopping, and I know Shon can't wait, either. How is he doing with all the shit going on with Koree?"

I had heard about Koree being raped and the shit hit home. I cried like a baby that whole night like I knew the girl. That shit was crazy. Then the sorry mutha fucker left her in the park knocked out. I was so pleased to hear that she was still alive for her daughter, but I knew from experience, it was a long road to recovery. Hell, my ass was still trying to recover.

"He's been out in the streets, trying to find who did this. He's been snapping on me and all types of shit. I've been letting him slide since I know why, and poor Kira has been whining for her mama." I felt bad for Erin. It sounded like she was going through a lot right now, but I knew no matter what, she would have Marshon's back because she loved him.

"Aww…pooh, I hope you're not stressing with my god baby baking in the oven."

"I'm a little stressed, but when everything becomes too much, I just call Mar's mama to watch the kids and I take a walk to clear my mind."

"So, what are the cops saying about all of this?"

"They think it's an outsider because it's been a long time since anything has happened like this in Atlantic County," Erin said, causing my mind to wander a little. I didn't know why Larry came to mind, but he did. I was glad I lived in Camden.

"Melani, what's wrong? You got quiet over there."

"Do you think Larry is in town? It's just a matter of time before he comes back to get his wife."

"You know what, Lani, I didn't even think about that. I'ma talk to Mar as soon as I get home about that. He gon' be mad I drove all the way down here, but I needed to get away. And I'm staying the night, too, just to let you know."

"Girl, you know damn well you don't have to tell me that. You're always welcomed. Besides, you just cursed me out for trying to put you out a minute ago, so I knew that wasn't going to happen."

"Exactly! Now, let's go find some snacks so we can work on your god baby's name. Of course, if it's a boy like Marshon says, he's going to be a junior. Now, if it's a girl, he left it up to us, and I figured you would love to help with this," Erin cooed.

"Oh my God! I would be honored, Erin!" I said, pressing my lips tight to keep from smiling all hard.

"Ya corny ass about to start cheesing all hard. Go find some snacks so we can get started. You know this is going to be an all-night thing, so we need to hurry up and get to it."

I headed into the kitchen to grab some snacks. I grabbed barbeque potato chips, Starburst that I had on the kitchen table, and a Pepsi for me. Then I grabbed Erin grapes, cheese, yogurt, and a bottled water. Once I retrieved everything, I went back into the living room with Erin. I noticed that she was on the phone, so I just signaled her that I was going to my bedroom.

I didn't know why, but the shit that happened to Koree kept playing in my head. I hated to think that Larry was in Atlantic City, but I had a gut feeling he was. As long as he stayed his black ass there, then I wouldn't have shit to worry about.

"Girl, I've been calling your ass. I turned the lights off since we are in here for the night. Are you OK? I was calling you loud as fuck, and I come in here and you just standing there in deep thought. What the hell is on your mind?" Erin asked, bringing me out of my thoughts. I swear I hadn't even heard her ass calling me. I didn't want to alarm her about how I felt. I also didn't want Javion and Marshon coming over here, forcing me to leave with them for my safety. It was a good thing I had gotten my gun and license to carry when I reached twenty-one. Erin didn't even know because I knew she would try to talk me out of it.

"I'm fine, just was thinking about all the work I have lined up. Did you and Mar decide if you were doing a gender reveal?" I asked, changing the subject.

"No, it's just too much going on. We just gon' have a big ass baby shower."

"Oh, all right, that's better anyway. I feel like the whole gender reveal is another way to spend money to party. They don't even bring gifts. If you had one, I was going to change the game. Whoever thought it was a boy, I was telling them to get a boy gift and vice versa. I was going to explain to them they must have gift receipts, so that way, you would be able to take the gifts back." Erin looked at me and started laughing.

"Lani, you a damn fool. Now that's doing way too much," Erin laughed.

"You know I'm extra and I'll do everything for my god kids and my own if I ever have any," I sighed.

"First of all, you said kids like I'm having a whole lot, and you're going to get your happy family one day, Melani, so stop talking like it's never going to happen. I told you, everything will fall into place when need be. Now, how come you got all the good snacks and gon' bring me this shit," Erin fussed, opening up my damn chips.

"You know you don't need all that damn salt. When ya feet be swollen, don't be complaining. Besides, grapes and cheese are good together."

"Well, you eat it and I'ma keep eating these chips," Erin said, waving a chip in my face. We sat up on my bed and talked half the night. We ended up with E'Lani Brielle for my god baby's name if it was a girl.

ζ*Chapter Twenty-One*ζ

Erin

Today was the day we found out what my peanut is, and I was so excited. Of course, Marshon wasn't here. He had gotten a phone call from Koree's step-pops that she was having an episode. I get that she had just gone through something and I couldn't imagine how she felt, but at the same time, I couldn't help but to get annoyed. Koree had a man, so why wasn't he handling her every need? It was like every time she called, or her stepdad called, Marshon would stop whatever he was doing. I'd had about enough of this, and we were going to talk about the issue today. At this point, I seriously believed that Koree was very aware of her actions and all she wanted was someone by her side. If her dude was there, she wouldn't want mine there all the time.

"OK, Mom, are you ready to do this, or do you wanna wait for Dad a couple more minutes?" the doctor asked.

"Yeah, we can get started. I don't wanna take up no more of your day. I know you have other patients that you need to get to. I would love to FaceTime my best friend so she can see everything."

"That is not a problem. Go ahead and lay down and pull your shirt over your belly, then call your friend as soon as you get comfortable."

I laid back then did everything the doctor told me to do. I was really getting upset that Marshon still hadn't walked through the door, but I already knew it was going to come to this since it had been like this for the past couple of weeks. I brushed my feelings to the side for a moment to dial Melani's number.

"Hey, pooh, you already at the doctor?" she answered in a joyful tone.

"Yes, I'm about to hit the FaceTime button. The doctor is ready to start."

The doctor placed the gel on my stomach, then got started. First, she should me his hurt and it was beating fine, then she showed me everything else. I was in awe seeing my little baby flutter around. The sound of sniffles brought me out of my thoughts.

"Melani, I know you're not crying."

"I know right. I can't believe you're going to be a mommy soon. I'm so excited for you, Erin."

"All right, ladies. Baby is doing fine and measuring fine. Now let's see what the sex of this bundle of joy is," the doctor said before moving the doppler around my belly.

Marshon still hadn't walked through the door yet, but Melani being on the phone with me kind of eased my mind a little. But, when I left this office, Mr. Shon was in for a rude awakening.

"All right, Mom, it looks like Dad was right; it's a strong, healthy baby boy. Congratulations to the both of you."

"Oh my God! Erin, we are having a boy!" Melani yelled into the phone. I couldn't do shit but laugh. Lani was happy from the beginning. She didn't care what the sex was, she just really wanted a baby around. I was mad as hell at Marshon, but I was happy to be giving him his first-born son. It really didn't matter what the sex was for me, I just wanted a healthy baby out the deal.

"Doc, can we keep the sex of the baby between us? If the daddy asks you, tell him I said no."

"You're the patient, it's whatever you want. I'm going to wipe your belly off now. Everything is fine with the baby so I won't need to see you until next month since you're doing great. Now remember, no stress, and if you have any problems, go to your local ER."

After the doctor left out, I got up to get myself together to leave out. I almost forgot Lani was on the phone until she spoke.

"Everything is going to be all right. He's going through some things right now, but y'all gon' be good."

"Lani, he missed a special moment that he will never be able to get back. I ain't trying to hear all that shit. I'ma call you later," I said, not giving her a chance to say anything else. I didn't need to hear Melani's shit. No matter what she said, Marshon was dead wrong for missing this appointment. I needed some time to myself, so I made my way out of the office. I didn't even get my paperwork for the next appointment. I figured I would just call later and have them fax it to our home.

Once I made it to the parking lot, I jumped in my car and peeled off. I always kept an overnight bag in my car so I knew I would be fine. I just didn't wanna stop by the house in case Marshon was there. I still couldn't believe he had missed this appointment.

******

I sat in my car for a second, debating if this was where I wanted to be. I knew he was pissed with me since I hadn't called him since the day Marshon came to my house, acting a damn fool. I had left the job and moved to Atlantic City without even letting him know, so I knew he was pissed with me. I knew I couldn't sit out here forever, so I got out of the car and eased my way up to his front porch. I then knocked on the door and got no response. I knocked a couple more times, but the last time, I noticed the curtains move. Norman was always petty, but today, I wasn't in the mood, so I turned around and headed back to my car. As soon as I opened the car door, I heard Norm yelling at me.

"Aht… aht…get ya ass back up here. You have no right to storm off and get back in your car. You the one that played me, so you should have just kept knocking until I decided to open the damn door. I don't know who the hell you think you are," Norman sassed, rolling his neck.

Even though I wasn't in the mood, he always seemed to put a smile on my face. I closed the door and then got my bag out of the trunk. I saw the way Norman was eyeing my bag and I knew he was going to say something smart. I walked up to him and pulled him in for a hug, and as soon as he hugged me back, I started crying. I needed a friend right now; I was so emotional at this moment. The situation may not have been serious to others, but to me, it meant everything, and I was hurt. Norman took my bag, then grabbed my hand and we walked into the house.

"I'm sorry I haven't called you. I know I should have given you a heads up that I was leaving the job, but I got wrapped up in my new life. After today, if you don't wanna deal with me, I'll understand, but I need a friend right now," I pleaded.

I stood there looking at Norman, waiting for a response. I just wished he would take it easy on my hormonal ass because this baby had me crying like crazy. Norman walked over to me and placed his hand on my belly.

"When did this happen? And is this why you left the job? Let me guess, Thug Life wanted you to quit your job so he can take care of you?" Norman sassed, rolling his eyes.

"No, that's not how it went down. I was already pregnant the day you were over the house, I just hadn't told anyone yet because I didn't know what I was going to do. I'm really sorry for leaving the job and not letting you know first. I really am, Norman."

"You didn't just leave the job, Erin, you moved away. I thought we were good friends. You just left and didn't tell me shit. You didn't even call or text. True friends don't do shit like that."

"I know, I know, and I promise I will never do anything like that to you again. Do you accept my apology?"

Norman got up and walked away from me. He headed into the kitchen and I didn't say anything, just sat there, looking crazy. After a couple of minutes, I decided to get up and make my way into the kitchen. When I got in there, he was taking everything out of the fridge to make a salad. Norman must have been really mad with me, he couldn't even answer me.

"I'm just gon' go ahead and leave," I said, turning to walk out.

"Man, Erin, I accept your apology, but if you pull some shit like that again, don't even come over here. Now sit ya ass down so I can feed my niece or nephew, and tell me what the fuck Thug Life done did. You already know I'm ready to beat his ass anyway.

Norman made me and him both a chicken caesar salad and I ran everything down. From the trip to Virginia to what was going on now. He sat there with his mouth wide open, but he gave some good advice. He even told me to apologize for hanging up on Melani and call her over to chill with us.

Today had been a hard day for me, but my friends were just what I needed to help me figure out what to do. I loved Marshon with all my heart, but he had to think about who came first in his life.

ϚChapter Twenty-TwoϚ

Marshon

The feeling of being tapped on my shoulder woke me from my deep slumber. I was sitting in the recliner that was in the corner of Koree's room. She wasn't doing too well after all that had happened to her, so I had been helping Mr. Gary keep her straight. I didn't know what was going on with Joe, but he should have been the one here helping her. I made a mental note to go talk to his ass as soon as I left here. I was beginning to fuck up at home. Erin didn't say shit, but I could see it all in her face. Between trying to get my business ventures in order and running back and forth over here, I was tired as shit, so I knew I was neglecting my girl in every way.

"Shon, are you hungry?" Koree asked, bringing me out of my thoughts.

"Girl, if you don't go lay down somewhere. I can get myself something to eat. What time is it?" I asked, looking outside, seeing that it was dark.

"It's about seven and your phone been ringing like crazy."

I picked my phone up off the table and saw I had a million phone calls from my mama. I hurried and dialed her number to make sure she was OK.

"'Bout time your ass answered. Y'all never came home from the doctor's appointment and I missed pocketbook bingo because I had the girls. I keep telling you, Marshon, I don't mind helping with my grandbabies, but when I have something to do, I need y'all to respect that. Now tell me what my new grandbaby is going to be. Is it a girl or a boy?"

"Oh shit, I missed the damn appointment. Mama, where is Erin?"

"I don't know, she never came home. Marshon, I know you lying about missing the appointment. That girl has been having a hard time dealing with you running to tend to Koree's every need. Don't she got her own man? I wouldn't be surprised if she wasn't doing all this on purpose. I'm not saying that what happened to her is a lie and that she's not going through something, but you have your own family over here and you need to get your shit together. Now call Melani and see if Erin is there because she never came here. If she takes my grandbaby away from you because you are being stupid, I'ma kick your ass. You better fix this shit," my mama snapped, then hung up in my ear.

"Koree, I have to go, ma."

"Shon, please don't leave me here alone. Gary went home to get some rest. I told him to go ahead because you were here."

"Well, I have to go. I'll get Joe to come over here."

"Joe don't love me anymore. He's embarrassed by what happened to me. I don't think he wants me anymore, Marshon," Koree said with tears running down her face. I couldn't help but to be sad about how she felt. I was going to stop my Joe's crib before I headed to the city to find Erin.

"That's not true, ma. He just going through a hard time out in these streets, trying to find out who did this to you. Joe is not trying to rest till whoever did this to you is dealt with. Let me go holler at him, and if he doesn't come back, then I will. Just watch some TV until one of us calls you, OK?" I sighed.

"All right, please don't be long. I don't like being here alone," Koree pleaded. At first, I thought my mama was right about her acting, but the shit she just said about Joe hurt my heart. This shit right here had me fucked up and the person who did this definitely needed to be dealt with asap.

I kissed Koree on her forehead and promised her someone would be back soon. I would always be there for all the mothers of my kids, but I was in love with Erin, and after I saw what the hell was going on with Joe, I would be going to look for my baby. After I locked up Koree's house, I hopped in my car and headed to Joe's crib.

Twenty minutes later, I pulled up in front of Joe's crib where he was sitting alone, smoking. I could tell he was in his feelings and had a lot on his mind. I jumped out my car, walked up on his porch and sat in the chair that sat across from him.

"What you doing here, Mar? If you came here to tell me I'm doing a poor job trying to find this mutha fucka that did this to my girl, I don't need you to. I already know I fucked up."

"Nah, man, I didn't come here for that. We gon' find out who did this shit and we gon' get his ass, but right now, Koree needs you. Do you wanna know what she said to me before I came here? She told me that you're embarrassed to be with her because this happened. She thinks you don't love her anymore."

Joe placed his face in his hands. I guess what I had just revealed to him had him fucked up. The way he was going hard to find out who did this to Koree made me believe that he really cared for her. At first, because of the Joe I remembered, I thought he was a total asshole. I'd recently learned that he had bought a couple of businesses to clean up his money. I also learned that the coke habit was just Koree's ass, and he promised me he was going to get her off of that shit.

"It's not like that, man. I really do love Koree, I just can't face her knowing that the nigga that did this to her is still out here. What kind of man am if I can't handle this nigga?"

"I get it, I really do, but she needs you by her side right now, then we will handle the person who did this. I just left her and she's in the house alone. I told her if you didn't come, I would come back, but I got some shit to handle with wifey, so I'm not going to be able to head back over there." Joe didn't say anything, he just pulled out his phone and called who I assumed was Koree.

"Hey, baby! I'm on my way over there. Do you need anything?" Joe spoke into the phone.

No other words needed to be said between Joe and I. We gave each other a head nod and I made my way back to my car. I was happy Koree had finally found someone who really loved her. Since my job was finished here, I jumped back in my car to hit the highway. My next stop was Melani's house.

*****

Forty-five minutes later, after doing ninety down the highway, I was standing in front of Melani's door like I was the damn police. I knew she was here because her car was parked.

"MELANI!" I yelled, probably waking her neighbors up, but I didn't give a fuck; she was going to answer me before I left. As soon as I was about to yell her name again, she opened the front door with the meanest mug on her face.

"Marshon, what the fuck are you doing here?" Melani snapped.

"You know why I'm here. Where the fuck is Erin at?"

"You should have thought about that before you missed the appointment today. I have never seen my friend this hurt. She is usually the one helping everyone. I'm not telling you where she is, now get the hell off my steps, Marshon. She loves you, so when she's ready to come home, she will. Right now, just leave her alone before you stress my god baby out."

Melani had me so pissed right now, and if my boy wasn't in love with her, I might have fucked her evil ass up, but I'ma chill. I had no idea where Erin could be since Melani was her only friend. I just dropped my head and walked my sad ass to the car. The thought of me wanting to know what the sex of my baby was came to mind, and I turned back towards Melani.

"What is it a girl or a boy?" I asked.

"None of ya damn business. Now, goodnight, Marshon," Melani said, slamming the door.

All I could do was shake my head. I decided to take my black ass back down the highway, but I knew one thing for sure; Erin didn't have long to bring her ass home before I did a nationwide manhunt.

ςChapter Twenty-Threeς

Liv

I had been calling Booby like crazy and, of course, this dude wasn't answering me, so I was annoyed. On top of that, Payne hadn't been keeping his hands to himself, and every time I called it off, he still popped up. He was really starting to scare me, which was why I needed to hurry up and get rid of Melani so Javion could save me from all of this.

"Liv, you don't hear me calling you? What you in here doing now?"

"Payne, please don't start with me. I was on the phone with the guy I had the meeting with. He's ready to start working with me."

I knew by the look on his face he was about to come at me with some bullshit. I never thought in a million years that Payne would be like this.

"Call him and tell him that you not working with him," Payne retorted.

"What do you mean, Payne?" I asked.

"I mean exactly what I said. I saw how that dude was all up on you and I don't want you working with him. I said what the fuck I said, Liv, damn. Why you always testing me, ma? You need to just start your own company and I'll help."

"Payne, how do you suppose I do that with no fucking money?"

"Go get it from daddy. You don't work for Javion no more, so I'm sure he will help you follow your dream of being a party promoter."

Payne just knew he knew what the fuck he was talking about, but didn't know shit. I didn't wanna be a promoter. Truth be told, I only took the job to be up under Javion. I saw him one day and just had to have him.

"My daddy isn't going to give me any money, Payne, so I don't know where you heard that from," I snapped, not expecting his fist the fly into my face.

"I don't know where you heard that from," Payne said, mocking me. "You gon' learn one of these days to do what the fuck I said and shut the fuck up. All you do is mouth off. Damn, just listen sometimes. You always making me do this to you. I wish you'd understand that I got you, so I'ma make sure you are doing everything right. I got your back, ma, just trust me. Now tell me about the pictures and other stuff that's in the envelope on your dresser. And don't

fix ya mouth to lie to me, either. I already did my research, I just wanna know what you have to say about all of this."

"It was nothing, Payne, just some shit I found out about Javion's uncle. I thought I would let him know, so that way, he would handle it before anyone else gets hurt," I managed to get out while still holding my face from when he punched me.

"I have a feeling you lying to me," Payne said, sitting next to me.

I knew he hated hearing anything about Javion, but it seemed like shit had been ten times worse since I had come back from Miami with a black eye, thanks to Melani's fat ass. Payne had this weird obsession with Javion, and to me, it was way more than jealousy. I knew he would be pissed with me, but I needed to ask.

"Why do you hate Javion so much?" I asked, swallowing a lump in my throat.

"Hmm…let's see. First of all, I always hated that nigga back in the day when we were in school. He thought he was big shit since his uncle ran the streets. Second of all, I couldn't stand how he treated you, but you just kept dropping ya draws for that nigga even though I tried to talk to you, and you would always push me away. Now I got you and Javion's name still in the mix. I don't know why you still want a nigga that don't want you. You be thinking a nigga dumb, but I done already put two and two together, and I know whatever you got going on with Javion's uncle has something to do with your own selfish reasons. Oh, and I been knowing you were lying from day one about that meeting. I knew who Booby was as soon as I saw him. That dude used to be one of the biggest OGs out here, so he is well known."

My eyes grew big as hell when he said he knew who Booby was ever since the night we met up. So, I knew he was pissed off because I had just lied again. I wasn't even going to lie, I was so scared right now. I tried to get up off the bed and Payne snatched me down by my hair.

"OUCH! Payne, please don't hurt me," I cried out.

"As long as you tell me what you were planning to do with all of this information, then I won't hurt you. I just need you to tell me the complete truth, that's it." I had a feeling that whether I told the truth or not, he was still going to hurt me, but at this point, I knew I couldn't get out of this shit.

"I just wanted her to hurt like she hurt me, so when I found out about Javion's uncle hurting her when she was younger, I figured why not send him back to her again to get even for what she did to my face."

"So, just because you got your ass beat, you were going to send a rapist to hurt someone whose life he already fucked up? You a cold bitch for doing some bullshit like that, Liv, when all you had to do was fight her again, flatten her tires, put sugar in her tank or some dumb shit like that. But not send a man to violate her. Now what were you going to do with the pictures of the chick laid out in the park? Who was she anyway?" Payne asked.

"I was using that picture for leverage since he had just done that a couple of days prior. That's Marshon's baby mama, Koree. She's also the girlfriend of this known drug dealer, Joe from Egg Harbor. If he didn't take care of Melani in a week, I was going to send them pictures to Marshon."

"Wow, Liv, you really are a sick person. So, you know about another woman being violated and you didn't have the sense to report it, because once again, all you care about are your own selfish reasons. I don't really fuck with Shon like that, but Joe and I go way back. I haven't talked to him in a minute, but I think I'll go visit him to tell him about this later. I'ma also call Javion to let him know that you sent his uncle to his girl's house. I bet after that, he really won't fuck with ya dumb ass anymore."

The tears ran down my face uncontrollably, hearing Payne say that. I knew if that shit got back to Javion, that would be it for me. I tried to get up again and Payne hit me so hard, I fell on the bed. Payne then grabbed my hands and handcuffed them to the bed pole and took the key.

"I can't have you trying to get away from me before I handle my business. And don't worry, Liv, I'm done with you. All I wanted to do was love and take care of you, but you got some serious issues. I know I need some help my-damn-self, but a woman that does some shit like this is bat shit crazy, and two crazy people will never work. Once I handle my business, I'll be back to let you loose," Payne said, leaving me in the room with a bloody face and tears falling. There was nothing else I could do, so I cried myself to sleep.

✶✶✶✶✶✶

The sound of noise in my room woke me. When I opened my eyes, my head started to throb instantly. I looked up and Payne was packing all of his shit that he had at my house, but the way he was moving was like he was in a rush.

"Baby, what are you doing? I thought we could work this out when you got back," I said in a sad tone. I really didn't think Payne was going to leave with the way he was obsessed with me. I guess what I'd done had really fucked with him. He didn't say shit after he gathered all his things and took them out of my room. I heard the front door open, so I assumed he was leaving. The crazy part was, he didn't even say anything, just grabbed his things and walked out. I heard footsteps and what sounded like two men entering my home, but neither of them sounded like Payne.

"Hey, Ms. Liv! How you, ma?" a tall, light-skinned dude with a low cut said when he entered my room. He had another dude with him that was kind of on the heavy side. He didn't say a word, he just stood there, looking crazy.

"Who are you, and where is Payne?" I asked in a nervous tone.

"Ma, I paid Payne and sent him on his way. See, I needed all the information that he gave me, and when he told me that you had this shit for over a week and didn't report it to Marshon or the police, I wanted ya ass gone just as bad as Booby's crack head ass. My girl been in the house crying, having nightmares, scared to come the fuck outside. This bitch ass nigga ruined her life. Then you keep his secret so he still running loose to hurt another woman. What happened to girl power?" he chuckled.

"Please don't hurt me. I'll do whatever you want me to do."

"I know you gon' do whatever I want you to. See, you about to write a whole letter saying that you took ya own life because both the men you wanted left you. Then Heavy over here is going to place the gun in your hand and help you end your miserable life. Ya time is up, baby girl. Next, we gon' get Booby's perverted ass."

The big dude walked over to the bed and uncuffed my hands. He then sat a pen and paper in my lap and sat next to me with the gun to my head. I began to write the letter. I had a whole bunch of shit running through my head. I might have been stupid over a man, but Javion was the love of my life and I guess since I couldn't have him, there was no need for me to live anymore.

ζ*Chapter Twenty-Four*ζ

Larry (Booby)

I had decided to lay low for a couple of weeks, but now it was time to handle what I needed to so I could get out of town. The crazy-ass bitch Liv kept calling me, so I figured I needed to do my homework on her ass. I found out that she was dating this abusive ass nigga named Payne. The crazy part was, she had just started out with him, so she didn't know his story. She was out here checking me when she should have been checking that nigga she was sleeping with. It was going to be easy as hell getting rid of her crazy ass. All I had to do was reach out to him and tell him she'd been trying to get with me. Dudes like him beat ass then ask questions.

"Yo, here you go, my man," the guy from the drug store said, handing me P's medicine. I had been staking out the front of her crib and noticed a dude was coming to drop medicine off. He didn't care what I did as long as the patient got her medicine, so I grabbed the bag and placed a baseball cap on my head, then made my way into her building. When I held the medicine bag up, the guard gave me the head nod to go in. I made it into the building and on to the elevator and thought, *Stupid assholes*.

Once I got to P's door, I knocked a couple times, then turned my back in case she looked out the peephole. That way, all she would see was the baseball cap since the dude that usually delivered her meds wore one. Just like I thought, she opened the door.

"Hey, Jerome, you're late today," she said, holding her hand out to get her medicine. As soon as I turned around, she looked at me as if she had seen a ghost.

"Well, hello, beautiful! You are looking good, baby," I said, pushing her into the apartment.

"Booby, what are you doing here? If they catch you in here, they'll kill you."

I stood there, staring at my wife. In such little time, she looked well. She still had a ways to go, but she definitely looked better.

"P, ain't nobody gon' kill me. I just came by to let you know that we are leaving the day after tomorrow. I have one more thing to do before I leave Jersey, then we can be on our way. I don't know why Javion thought he was going to just bring you over here and I don't have no say so. They could have given you the money to take care of your treatments down in Virginia."

"Yeah OK, Booby. You know damn well what would have happened if they would have given me money for my treatments. Your ass would have smoked it all up like you did all the rest of our money, remember? Now you better get the hell out of here before the guard come. It doesn't take this long to drop medicine off."

Porsha was in a mood today and I didn't like it. I couldn't believe these assholes had turned my fucking wife against me. Her ass was leaving with me even if I had to drag her mutha fucking ass out of this apartment. I walked up in her face and looked her dead in her eyes.

"I don't know what them little niggas put in your head while you were down here, but I'm not about to do this with you. Like I said, we are going back to Virginia the day after tomorrow. Even if I have to drag you out or kill them little niggas, I will. Don't make this hard, P."

"All right, Booby…please just leave before it's a problem." As soon as she said that, there was a knock at the door. I knew it was the guard because I was taking too long.

"Answer that shit and make sure you tell him that I had to thoroughly check this time because last time, the other dude brought the wrong medicine."

Porsha went to open the door. I knew she didn't want any problems, so she was going to do what I told her. As soon as she opened the door, the guard walked in and I walked out.

"Sorry he took so long, JT. We had to go through all the meds to make sure they were right this time," Porsha lied.

"OK, Ms. P, I was just doing my job," the guard said, giving me a head nod. Once I was out of the door, I hurried out of there then peeled off. I didn't know what P was capable of because that person wasn't my wife.

I was on my way to get something to eat, then I was going to Jersey. It was time I met up with Ms. Melani. We had some issues we needed to resolve since she was never supposed to open her mouth about what happened in her childhood to anyone. Then she comes along and tells my nephew of all people. The little bitch messed up my family like she almost did when she was younger. Her running away from home when she was thirteen had a nigga scared. I had so much back then, and my shit was running smoothly. I felt like if I hadn't left Jersey, shit would have stayed straight for me, but this little young bitch had fucked shit up then, too.

*****

I had been sitting in my car down the street from Melani's crib for hours. I knew she was in there alone because I saw her when she came home. Since her lights had been off for about an hour, I knew she was probably asleep by now. I hurried and got out of my car, put a black ski mask on my face, then went around the back of her place so I could figure out how to get in. Once I made my way to the back, I saw she had left the kitchen window unlocked. I eased it up and made my way into her home.

When I got all the way in, I moved around in silence, checking everything out before I made my way into the bedroom. The place was clean, and it smelled so good. Baby girl was totally different from her coked-out mama. Melody wasn't good for shit but sucking and fucking. Bitch couldn't even cook.

After I finished looking around, I made my way up the steps to her bedroom, trying not to make too much noise. When I made it to her bedroom, I stood in the doorway and watched her sleeping with the covers over her face. Baby girl was fully covered like she was freezing her ass off. I walked over to the bed, and as soon as I leaned over to move the covers so I could see her face, she jumped up and slapped the shit out of me, causing me to lose my footing.

"I didn't think you were going to stoop this fucking low, but when I heard what you did to Koree, I knew this was your next stop. So, I told Javion and Marshon to let me handle this. I can't believe you, Booby. Why? Just tell me why. What, I wasn't woman enough for you? I didn't suck ya dick good or fuck you good enough? What made you go out and do these things to these women? Even back when you touched Melani. When we were together, I knew you were cheating with Melody, but I didn't know you were touching her baby. She was a little ass girl, Booby," my wife said, now standing up on the side of the bed with a gun pointed at me.

I was so in shock; she had caught me off guard. When did she get here? I didn't see anyone but Melani come in. The look on my wife's face was doing something to a nigga, and I knew the shit was hard for her, too.

"Come on, P. What are you doing with that gun pointed at me?"

"NO, BOOBY! You don't get to ask me shit. I'm the one asking the questions right now," she screamed while the tears ran down her face.

"Baby, I'm sorry. I got problems and I need some help. I need you to come back home with me so I can get some help. Are you willing to do that for me? I promise I'm going to get myself together."

"I may be willing, but I need to ask you something, and I need the truth."

"Everything is already on the table, so whatever you wanna know, I got you," I said, being truthful.

"Was it you that raped them girls in Virginia? When the serial rapist was going around?"

I hated to tell her the truth about this, but if it was going to get her to leave and go home with me, I was all for it.

"Yes, it was me, and I'm sorry. I told you I need help, so come on, baby, put the gun down and we can leave. We need to go now before Javion and them get here. You know they not gon' leave you alone too long. How did you get here anyway?"

"I know you didn't think I was going to let her come do this by herself," Javion said, walking into the room with Melani next to him.

"I see, and you got ya fat bitch with you," I chuckled, causing Melani to run over to me and punch me right in the mouth. Little baby hit me hard as shit and I could taste the blood in my mouth.

"Be thankful for your wife wanting to talk, because if it was me lying in that bed, I would have killed ya ass as soon as you stepped foot in my house. Ever since I saw you again in Virginia, I wanted to find you and kill you, but thanks to my therapist, I figured I would leave it alone. She tells me daily that I need to forgive and then I can go on with life. So, it's time for me to forgive and let go so I can let Javion love me properly," Melani babbled. I didn't give a fuck what she was saying. While everyone was listening to her sob story, I tried to charge at Porsha, thinking she wasn't paying attention to me.

Pow...Pow...

P let off two shots, hitting me dead in the chest. I fell straight to the floor. I was so shocked that my wife had shot me. After I fell, she ran over to me and kneeled on the floor.

"You won't be able to hurt no one ever again, including me. Goodbye, Booby," Porsha said, letting off another shot in my head.

ʓ*Chapter Twenty-Five*ʓ

Melani

The sunlight shining in my face woke me from my deep slumber. Considering how last night went, I was sure I wouldn't be able to sleep. Being in Javion's arms all night played a big part. Booby being gone also helped. The man who haunted me most of my life was finally gone and I had the chance to talk to him face to face before he died. I needed that more than I thought I did.

"Good morning, beautiful, are you hungry?" Javion asked, walking over to the bed to sit next to me.

"Yeah, I'm a little hungry. How are you feeling this morning?"

"I'm good, baby. As long as you're here with me, I'ma be straight," Javion beamed, leaning in to kiss my forehead. I knew this was hard for him and his Aunt P. A situation like this had to be hard on anyone, so I made him promise if he needed to go to counseling to let me know and he promised he would.

Javion and I managed to finally talk when him and Aunt P showed up at my house to tell me about Booby being in town. As soon as Erin told me what happened to Koree, I had a strong feeling it was Booby and wasn't surprised when they told me it was him. It took Booby forever to make a move, so while we waited, Javion and I stayed in my guest room and talked in the dark for hours. He even told me the plan that Liv had put in motion. I couldn't believe that chick was really going crazy over this man. I didn't ask what happened to her because I really didn't care at this point.

It was something about the way he was ready to kill his uncle over me that had me thinking this man was seriously in love with me. Right then and there, I knew he was the one. Not to mention, he had been calling, texting, and sending me cards and flowers ever since we came back from Miami. Javion could have given up on me a long time ago, but he didn't. When I found out Booby was his uncle, I felt like I was messing up a happy family with the way he always talked about his uncle. Then after hearing Aunt P's story, I didn't feel bad for him at all after that. She had been hurting for years, dealing with suspecting that her husband was a rapist. Because of her loving him as much as she did, she said she ignored all the signs. I felt bad for her, but with therapy and her being here with people who loved her, she would be just fine.

"Melani, you good, ma?" Javion asked, bringing me out of my thoughts.

"Yes, I'm OK, I was just in my thoughts. Can you come with me to see Cliff today?" I asked Javion.

I knew since I'd finally forgiven Melody and Larry, I needed to forgive the man who made me. I'd had time to think, and it was about time I made shit right with him. We were all we had, and I would love to finally have a family that loved me.

"Of course, I can go with you. I'm so glad you decided to go, but I thought Erin was going with you."

"She was supposed to go, but your bro won't let her out of his sight. You know he went over Norman's house, acting a damn fool the day after he came over my house, acting up." I giggled because Shon was a damn fool over Erin's ass.

"Wait, what? He didn't tell me that. How did he even find out where dude lived?"

"He went up to the job and scared the address out of the human resource lady. He probably caused that lady to lose her damn job," I said, shaking my head.

"Yo, he's a damn fool, but I'm glad they good now. I'm even happy Koree is doing better and Joe is by her side. I know things between us aren't one hundred yet, but I'm going to do everything in my power to make sure you're treated the way you should be treated. We can take it slow like you wanted to and as long as you need to. I know you still battling things within yourself and it's going to take time to love me the way I love you."

Javion was right. I was still dealing with some things, but what he didn't know was I already loved him the way he loved me.

"I may be still battling with some things, but Javion, don't ever think I don't love you the way you love me because I do. In such a little time, you have shown me so much about myself. You make me feel beautiful every day, and when you walk in the room, even when you piss me off, I feel butterflies in my stomach. Baby, I already love you, and I'm wishing for a couple of forevers with you," I cooed while leaning in to kiss his soft lips.

I know we weren't where we needed to be, but if he kept treating me the way he had been treating me, it wouldn't take long at all. I finally had Javion Banks back in my presence, and I was the happiest girl in the world.

******

Javion and I were standing outside of Cliff's house, knocking on the door. He wasn't answering and I was getting concerned, so I told Javion to go through the front window that was opened. Just like I thought, when Javion opened the door, Cliff was lying on the couch in a deep slumber. His house was a damn mess and it smelled like the front of the Camden Transportation Center.

"CLIFF! CLIFF!" I yelled two times, slapping him on his arm.

"Hello, Elise, is that you?" he had the nerve to ask, trying to sit his drunk ass up.

"No, it's Melani, Cliff. Javion is going to help you upstairs to take a shower while I clean up a little. Baby, can you help him up to get cleaned up for me?" Javion gave me a head nod, letting me know he had me covered.

As soon as Javion got Cliff upstairs, I made my way into the kitchen to see if there were any trash bags and cleaning supplies. On my way to the kitchen, I noticed how nice the dining area was. When I walked into the kitchen, it was nice as well. The living room must have been where Cliff had been spending his days. The big ass picture that resided on their dining room wall had me feeling a little bit jealous. It was a picture of Cliff, his wife, and Elise, looking like one big happy family.

"You not here for that. Remember you here to forgive so y'all can go on with the future," Javion said, scaring the shit out of me.

"Shit, Javion, you scared the hell out of me."

"I'm sorry, but I saw your face all tore up when you looked at the picture. Cliff was wrong for how he did things, but you have to understand he was battling demons he never wanted to face again. Baby, just give him a chance. I want you to be happy, and you always being sad and holding things in makes it hard for me to make you happy."

Javion was right, if I wasn't going to do this for Cliff, I at least had to do it for my peace. J started cleaning while I put a pot of coffee on for Cliff since I knew he probably had a major headache.

After we finished cleaning, Cliff was finally coming back downstairs. He looked around and saw that his house was clean. I handed him the mug of black coffee and he took a sip, then sat down in the recliner.

"Thank you, Melani! I'm sorry you had to come here to see me like this. I'm just losing my mind around here. I don't think I'm able to live without my family. I feel like losing them was my karma for leaving you without a daddy. I'm so sorry for that, and if you never wanna forgive me for that, then that's fine with me. I'll leave you alone and leave you to your life, but I need you to do one thing for me. I need you to continue to run the boutique for me."

I sat there in awe, knowing that he wanted me to run the boutique, but I had my own thing going on. I didn't mind helping him run it, but I wasn't going to run it alone.

"Cliff, what happened to your family was unfortunate, but I don't think it was your karma. Sometimes, God makes decisions that we don't understand, but always know He doesn't make mistakes. Also remember that He forgives everyone. Now, I'm here today because I wanna forgive you. As far as us having a future together, I'm willing to take baby steps. All I ask is that you give me my space and wait till I'm ready. I will also help you run the boutique, but I will not do it alone. That is your place of business, and you need to get out of this funk and get back to it. I have my own business I started, so sometimes, I won't be able to be at the boutique. If you need me, I will help with hiring and ordering supplies so we can get everything set back up for business since it's been closed for a minute.

Me, Cliff, and Javion sat and talked for hours. I told Cliff about my styling business and I also told him I wanted to start my own clothing line. We laughed, we cried, and we promised each other that we would work on our father-daughter relationship. The past couple of days had been something, but for the first time in my life, I saw peace and happiness in my future.

Epilogue
Six months later

Melani

"Aunt P, everything is already set up. I wish you'd go sit down somewhere," I sassed. We were getting ready for Erin and Marshon's sip and see. Erin had gone into the hospital before she was able to have the baby shower, so we canceled it and decided to do this. MJ was now two months since he was born early.

"Girl, don't tell me what to do. It's been so long since I've been able to do anything without feeling sick," Aunt P yelled. She was in remission and we were all happy about that. After Booby passed and she had to handle all the arrangements since she was his wife, Aunt P went into a dark space that we had to help her out of since her health wasn't the best. With plenty of prayer and therapy, we got her right. I'd even introduced her to Cliff. Even though they were both recovering from losing their spouses, they had become good friends and we thought that was what was keeping them out of their dark places. Javion had a couple of episodes, but he quickly recovered. There were some things he needed to get off his chest. Losing his parents then his uncle who raised him was hard, but he was fine now and enjoying life. Marshon, on the other hand, hated Booby for what he did to Koree, and if Aunt P hadn't killed Booby, he would have. A couple days after everything went down, I saw on the news that Liv had taken her own life and left a suicide note. I knew it probably wasn't true, but I didn't read too much into it. I just left it alone and went on with life.

"All right, auntie, I'ma let you live today," I giggled, walking away. On my way into the kitchen, I saw Koree and Joe walking up. Koree was doing well. I had introduced her to my therapist, and it was helping. I even started taking her to support groups with me. It was even helping her and Erin with their relationship. At first, Erin and Koree were having a hard time co-parenting, but now things were great. I think Koree just needed her own man so she could stop stalking Marshon. As for the other baby mama, they never had any problems out of her.

"Hey, girl, how you?" Koree asked, pulling me in for a hug.

"I'm good, boo, just trying to finish getting everything set up before they get here. You can put your gifts over on the gift table," I directed Koree.

"Hey, Lani, where Javion at?" Joe asked.

"The men are in the den. You know how they be."

Joe headed to the den, while Koree and I walked into the kitchen. Koree stood off to the side, admiring my kitchen. This was actually the first time Javion and I were having something at our new house. Yeah, y'all heard right. I decided to move down here with him. He didn't want me to move into the house he already had. He wanted me to pick out my dream house, then he sold his and purchased this one.

"This home is beautiful, Lani. Javion outdid himself with this one. So, how y'all been doing? You still taking things slow?" Koree whispered. She knew I had been holding out on Javion sexually from our many talks. I looked at her and smiled, and she started jumping up and down.

"Yes, finally, and it was beautiful just like all of you told me. I've never experienced anything like that before in my life. It was well worth the wait."

"I'm sure it was. When two people who love each other explore each other's bodies, it's the best feeling ever. I'm so happy for you, girl, and I wanna thank you for helping me through my rough time. I'm finally getting myself together, and Joe has been amazing," Koree beamed.

"That's good, girl. Now help me get all this food into the dining room."

Koree and I set everything up and all the guests were starting to arrive. I didn't even know Marshon knew all these damn people. I knew Erin didn't really deal with anyone but me and Norman, who was in the living room, laughing with Aunt P and Marshon's mama.

"Hey, suga!" a familiar voice said from behind. I was so excited to hear Blu's voice. I had been so busy with moving, the boutique, and Style's by Lani, I hadn't even had time to visit my friend.

"Oh my God! Hey, baby! I missed you so much. We have to catch up now that I live out here. Where is LaMir?"

"Now you know he was texting Javion on our way here, so he went straight to the den. This house is everything, and who does y'all landscaping?" Blu asked.

"Whoever your husband recommended," I laughed. Javion, Marshon, and LaMir had been working together on some business ventures. LaMir got them hooked up in the hotel business. A lot of the hotels were closed and being renovated, so LaMir hooked them up with his brother Liam so they could look into buying one apiece. They both so happened to be on each side of LaMir's casino, so between that, J. Banks Entertainment and Style's by Lani, money was rolling in. I even had a couple of business ventures going myself. I was finally going to meet with a fashion designer this week to sell my sketches, too, so I could start my new clothing line, which would be named Curvy Styles. I would also be the one modeling my clothing alongside Nubia Lee. This had been a dream of mine since I was younger.

"The star has arrived." I heard Erin's loud mouth, so I had to run to see my god baby.

"Hey, my fat man!" I cooed, snatching the baby out of her arms.

"Damn, that's all you see?" Erin said before she looked around and saw the decorations. Her eyes lit up and she leaned in and kissed my cheek. I smiled at her and headed into the living room to show Aunt P the baby.

"Nope, hoe, give me my nephew," Norman yelled as soon as I hit the living room. He tried to take the baby out of my arms, but Aunt P pushed him out of the way.

"Y'all better not drop my grandson or I'ma beat y'all all up," Mar's mama said, causing us all to laugh. She was so attached to all of Marshon's kids, but the way she was with this grandson was something different. Erin said sometimes she had to remind her that it was her baby. On another note, I was so happy for Erin. She had this mother thing on point while still doing her school thing. She had one more year left, then she would be finished, so things were going well with everyone and life was grand. It took a lot for me to get where I was today, and I was the happiest girl in the world.

"Hey, y'all, I need everyone to come in the dining room for a minute. I wanna do a toast before the party gets started," Javion yelled to get everyone's attention. Erin and Aunt P looked at me and I hunched my shoulders, letting them know I didn't know what this was all about. When I made it into the dining room, I stood in front of him and he leaned in to kiss my lips. I knew he had something up his sleeve, but I just didn't know what.

"What's going on, baby?" I asked, curious.

"I wanted to thank everyone for coming out. Erin and Marshon, I wanna say congratulations on your new bundle of joy. I also wanna thank the two of you for allowing me and Melani to be the godparents. I love you both, and I wish you many years of love together. I'm not trying to steal y'all shine today, but this is something I needed to do while everyone was in attendance," Javion said, kneeling on one knee. Before his knee even hit the floor, I screamed yes.

"Girl, let the boy ask the damn question," Aunt P yelled, causing everyone to laugh.

"Melani, baby, we had a rough start, but I was never going to rest until I got you. I didn't care how much you pushed me away, I was coming back. All I wanted to do from the moment I met you was love you and make you happy. You've changed my life so much, and I want nothing more than to spend the rest of my life with you. Melani, will you marry me?" Javion asked with sweat pouring down his forehead.

"Yes, Javion! Yes, I will marry you." Javion got up and I pulled him in for a hug. Once I was in his arms, we kissed like we were in the room alone. Everyone clapped, yelled, and cheered us on. Today was the happiest day of my life, and I finally felt complete. I finally felt free. I finally felt at peace. It may have taken going through some changes. But, Melani Clark was finally living the life that she had always dreamed of.

The End...

Are you in search of a good publishing home?
Tyanna Presents just may be the perfect place for you!

We are currently accepting submissions in the following genres:

URBAN FICTION
URBAN ROMANCE
WOMEN'S FICTION
STREET LIT
BWWM
PARANORMAL
EROTICA
SUSPENSE

For consideration, please submit the first 3 chapters of your manuscript to:

TYANNAPRESENTS1@GMAIL.COM

Join my Facebook reading group: Tyanna's Literary Divas